BADGER CREEK

JOHN HANSEN

BADGER CREEK
Published through SUMMIT CREEK PRESS

Dedication: To Debi, my wife and forever partner.

The characters and events portrayed in this book are fictitious.
Any similarity to real persons, living or dead, is coincidental
and not intended by the author.

ISBN: 978-0-578-84135-9

CHAPTER ONE

I adjusted my reading glasses so as to be able to read the form on my desk. Anymore, all print was fine print. I was elaborating, as the District Attorney had asked, on whether the empty Coors can in Luther Nye's pickup had contributed to him missing a curve out on County Road 29 and rolling his truck several times before coming to rest on its top but minus Eloy Snyder. As luck would have it, I was the first one to happen upon the wreck. The cab of Luther's pickup was smashed down pretty good and both doors had popped open. It looked like anyone inside it wouldn't have survived but there was Luther, bloody face and all, staggering around in the sagebrush mumbling something about how he'd *hit that new oil and the ass end of my pickup just slid out from under me.* I'd noted the fresh asphalt and the loose gravel but didn't think it was a real hazard other than a person could get a cracked windshield if they met another car that was going too fast. I recalled, as I stepped off the pavement and started towards Luther's pickup that the radio was still playing. Johnny Cash was singing *Ring of Fire.* My route to the pickup was meandering on account of the sage being about three feet tall. When I was about fifteen feet from the pickup and Luther, my eyes sent a painful dose of adrenaline through my body. It caused me to jump back a bit before embarrassment over-rode my shock. Protruding from beneath the crushed cab of the truck were a pair of black cowboy boots with a leafy red and blue design that began at the ankle and disappeared into the legs of some new looking Levis. I stood still, like I was as dead as Eloy Snyder and ran my eyes up the legs to a big silver belt buckle with a bucking bull on it that was partially hidden by the green Dodge. At about this time Johnny Cash was singing *I went down, down, down and the flames went higher.* It used to be that song took me to the American Legion bar and Ellen and I having dinner and dancing, but not anymore. Across the room I heard the phone ring and Millie answering it.

"Oh, my goodness. I'm so sorry."

Millie's end of the conversation crowded the image of Luther's wreck out of my mind. It appeared that she was genuinely disturbed by what was being told to her.

"Just one moment, Sir. I'll let you talk to the Sheriff."

Millie looked over at me. I could see through her cat eye glasses that her green eyes had puddled up and were on the verge of overflowing. She said, almost simultaneous to the phone on my desk ringing. "Andy, this is Fred Bolander. It isn't good."

I knew Fred from high school but that had been 25 years ago. He was one of those quiet kids, not into sports or the social mainstream at school. We weren't really what you'd call friends as I hung out mostly with the jocks and he did not. We'd nod or say hi to one another in the hall or during deer season we might exchange hunting stories. What I remember most about Fred was the blue jacket he seemed to wear a lot. Across the back were gold letters that read, Future Farmers of America. After graduation he went to work on his family's ranch north of town. I'd heard that the place was his now. I sighed and picked up the phone. "Mornin' Fred. What can I do for ya?"

From the phone there was a few seconds of silence and then what sounded like someone trying not to sob, but he did.

I glanced over at Millie who was dabbing at her nose with a Kleenex while looking at me. Her anguish coupled with Fred's inability to even speak, and far in the back of my mind Johnny Cash singing *Ring of Fire* for an unresponsive Eloy Snyder, caused my heart to ratchet up a notch. I felt as if I was about to open a box of rattlesnakes. Nonetheless, I said with compassion, "What's happened, Fred?"

The sobbing abruptly stopped. "Some dumb sonovabitch killed my boy."

I was taken aback by the intense anger in his voice. It was difficult for me to associate the voice with the Fred I knew but then I said, "Who killed your boy? I mean, how did this happen?"

A slightly calmer Fred came back. "Me and Teddy went out to the Gros Ventre this morning to cut some posts. I got a permit from the forest service to cut lodgepole up Badger Creek. We'd barely got started when Bosco wandered off."

"Bosco?"

"Yeah, Teddy's dog. He loves that animal. We'll be workin' cattle out in the mountains and that dog goes outta sight more an' a few minutes and Teddy will start fretting about it and go hunt him down. Most every time he'll find him sitting next to a tree staring up at a squirrel that is chattering away. It always made Teddy laugh. So today when he went looking for Bosco, I figured it was the same situation and the both of them would be back in a few minutes. I was running the saw falling and bucking trees so I guess I got distracted, but the next thing I know is Bosco comes running up to me and the end of his nose is laid open and he's bleeding. Right away I figure something's happened cuz Teddy ain't with him. So, I no sooner shut the saw off and Bosco barks at me and heads back up the hill into the timber. I take out after him and –." The phone went silent for a moment and then I heard Fred take a deep breath and let it out. He went on, "About three hundred yards into the trees I found Teddy. Bosco took me right to him."

"What happened to him, Fred?"

"He was shot in the chest."

"Shot? Are you sure?"

"Hell yes, I'm sure. The gun was right there tied to a tree."

Instantly, I knew what had likely happened. "A set gun? Those things are illegal."

"Well, it's still up there tied to an Aspen tree. It's an old Winchester 30-30. His setup with the string tied to the trigger and the staple in the tree and the meat for bait, it's all there."

I knew Fred had to be in the little town of Cedarville since that was the only place in the Gros Ventre River valley where there was a phone. Knowing the answer that I would probably get, I asked, "And Teddy?"

Fred's response was quick and curt. "Him and Bosco are with me. I'm headed to O' Leary's funeral home and the vet, in that order. If you need to talk to me some more that's where I'll be."

"This is a crime, Fred. I need to go to where it happened."

"My wife doesn't know yet. After I tell her she's going to need me."

"Sure Fred, I understand. Do you suppose you could draw me a map?"

"Yeah, I can do that. I'll be at O'Leary's in about a half hour."

"Alright, I'll meet you there."

Fred hung up before I could tell him that I was sorry for his loss. I suspected that right now words, any words, wouldn't matter much. It had seemed that way a week ago when I'd gone into the Rexall Drug store to tell Lyla Snyder that her husband was dead. My, *I'm sorry for your loss* had, it seemed, only reinforced the fact that she would be alone now. Her legs had begun to buckle. She might have collapsed to the floor had the pharmacist and I not helped her to one of the round stools at the soda bar.

"So, I guess after the funeral home you'll be going on out to the Gros Ventre?" asked Millie.

I looked over the counter in front of our desks to the clock on the wall. It was a quarter till twelve. I tried unsuccessfully to not frown before saying, "I'll be late gittin' back. Badger Creek is pretty far up the Gros Ventre. Radio reception is kinda iffy up there so just remember that if you can't git ahold of me. Probably gonna be seven o'clock or so when I git back to town."

"You want me to call Tyler and let him know where you're headed to?"

Tyler Cummins was my deputy, my only deputy. He was 24, not much older than I had been when I started with the Gros Ventre County Sheriff's Department nearly 24 years ago. I said, "Yeah, probably wouldn't be a bad idea just in case somebody needs to come lookin' for me."

Millie's mother hen side came out as she shot back real quick like, "You ain't expecting trouble out there, are you?"

I laughed. "No, it's just my boy scout training kicking in I guess."

Millie scowled and dashed her head to the side as if to emphasize what she was about to say. "You laugh, Andy, but you should know better than anybody that some of them people in that valley are just plain ornery."

"I like to think we've weeded out the worst ones."

Millie scoffed, "Yeah, well I think your garden just keeps sprouting more weeds."

I smiled so she would know that I appreciated her concern and said "I guess I better skedaddle." And then I started towards the door that opened to the hallway that ran in front of our three jail cells and on out the back door of the office. My hand had just settled on the doorknob when Millie called out, "You want me to call Ellen and let her know you'll be late?"

I paused and looked over at Millie. "I don't know. She went to some big forest service confab over in Bozeman yesterday. She thought she'd be home before quittin' time today so you might give her a call just short of five o'clock."

"She's sure done well with that outfit," replied Millie in a tone that suggested she had momentarily forgotten Fred Bolander's call.

I nodded. "Yes mam, she has. Receptionist to Admin Officer. There ain't a nickel spent on that forest that she doesn't know about."

And then Millie seemed to step totally away from the emotion that had gripped her just a few minutes ago. She said, "Her having that good paying job must take some of the pressure off of you winning this election."

I hoped Millie meant well and wasn't fishing for gossip. Regardless, I ignored her probe and said simply, "I better go."

CHAPTER TWO

Raymond O'Leary was a young guy, in his mid-thirties I'm guessing, who moved to Fremont from Billings about five years ago and opened of all things, a funeral home. To do this in a town of 1,752 people seemed strange to the residents as Fremont already had a funeral home that had been in business for over 50 years. People are prone to go with someone they know and that wasn't Raymond. Things got so bad for him that he was finally forced to take a part-time job at the CO-OP. It was as good a place as any to meet potential customers for his business but still, he struggled to make ends meet. Then, his ship came in. About a year ago the county coroner just up and quit. Raymond applied and got the job on an interim basis until this fall's election. Being an employee of the county myself, I knew that he wasn't getting rich on the coroner's salary, but the job seemed to give him more justification for being in Fremont than just *running the new guy's funeral home.* On the drive across town I envisioned the emotional dilemma that he would be in with the arrival of Fred and Teddy's body. On the one hand, he would be selling a funeral and proving that he was capable of performing the duties of coroner. As morbid as these events were, they would reduce the stress in Raymond's life and lighten his usual demeanor. On the other hand, however, to display anything but a totally somber expression in the presence of Fred might not bode well.

As I pulled up to the funeral home, I saw Raymond come out of the side door and get into the hearse which was parked under the carport. It was an older model black Cadillac that he had bought used up in Great Falls. When he started it up, a small cloud of blue smoke initially spewed out of the exhaust. After gunning the motor a few times, it mostly dissipated as he pulled the car around to the rear of the building. Moments later he came back. I met him under the car port.

"Good morning, Sheriff,"

"Mornin," I said as I shook his outstretched hand. "I suspect Fred ought to be here anytime."

"I'm surprised, as mad as he was on the phone."

"Whaddaya mean?"

"He didn't tell you about the sheepherder?"

"No, he never said a word."

Raymond's demeanor suddenly became a little guarded. "Well, I don't know if I shouldn't let Fred tell you."

I looked hard at Raymond. He was a slender guy, kind of mousey with short red hair and dressed all the time like he was on his way to church. I said, in a no non-sense tone, "For hell sakes, Raymond. You being a county official should come before you pissin' off a customer. So, what about this sheepherder?"

Raymond momentarily pursed his lips and then sighed. "I guess when Fred was coming out of Badger Creek he ran into a sheepherder that was pushing a big bunch of sheep across the bottom of the canyon. They had the road blocked. He said the longer he sat there waiting for those sheep to move the more convinced he was that he was likely looking at the guy that had killed his son."

Raymond paused like he was reluctant to go on.

"And then what?" I said.

Raymond sighed again. "Well, he said he got out of his truck and confronted the herder. Said the guy was Basque and didn't speak much English and well – I guess things just got out of hand."

"Out of hand?"

"Yeah, he said he gave the guy a good beating and left."

It was hard for me to imagine Fred giving anybody a beating as he was about six inches shorter than me, but then I'd never had to carry my dead son's body out of the woods only to run smack dab into a guy who was a prime candidate as his killer. I said, "He didn't say anything more about the herder's condition?"

"No, he was semi-hysterical. He was talkin' a hundred miles an hour."

And then, before I could question Raymond any further, I saw from the corner of my eye a red Chevy pickup come almost to a complete stop at the railroad tracks up the road. The driver eased the vehicle over the bumpy strips of steel like he was carrying a load of eggs and then gradually accelerated. Seconds later I could see that it was Fred. He came on, never getting beyond third gear, until finally he slowed and turned towards us coming to a stop under the carport. As I stepped up to the driver's window, I could see the outline of a body beneath a blanket in the bed of the pickup. A black and white dog lay next to the body with its head resting on its paws. He raised his head slightly and looked at me but did not bark. Fred seemed frozen behind the wheel. His blue eyes, as one might expect, were bloodshot. He sat there with his hands, stained with the blood of his son and some no doubt the sheepherder, gripping the wheel. He appeared unable to get out and do what came next.

I said, "I'm so sorry for your loss, Fred. It ah, it ain't right."

He looked over at me from beneath the brim of his dirty, sweat stained, straw cowboy hat. The sadness that radiated from his face was crushing. He said, "No, it ain't. We just went up there to cut some posts and now look where we're at."

On the other side of the truck, I heard the clatter of the gurney's wheels as Raymond pulled it out the side door of the funeral home and around to the back of the vehicle. In the rearview mirror, Fred saw what was about to happen. He shouted, "Hold on, I'll git 'im." And with that he bailed out of the cab. I stepped back as he lowered the tailgate. He started to cry as he looked down at his son. For a moment he looked as if he wouldn't be able to do it, but then he said softly to the dog, "C'mon Bosco, you gotta let Teddy go." But the dog continued to lay where he was with his head resting on the boy's body. Tears were clearly running down Fred's cheeks and his nose had begun to run. He swept the back of his hand across his upper lip and both sides of his face as if this would allow him to regain his composure, but it did not.

Seeing that Teddy was wrapped in a colorful patchwork quilt but laying on a new canvas irrigation dam, I surmised that Fred must have gotten these items from the owner of the Cedarville store. I moved next to him. "How 'bout I give you a hand?"

He gently bobbed his head like he was in a daze and then whispered. "All right."

I reached into the bed of the pickup and grabbed the edge of the canvas with both hands and began to pull. The movement caused Bosco to stand but not get off of the canvas. One good pull and Teddy's feet were at the edge of the tailgate. Fred suddenly came to life. He said, "I've got him now." And then he leaned in and scooped his son up, holding him for a long moment before gently placing him on the gurney.

There was genuine sadness in Raymond's face as he made eye contact with Fred. He said, his voice barely above a whisper, "I'll take good care of him, Mr. Bolander."

Fred's composure suddenly returned. "There ain't no mystery as to what killed Teddy. He was shot. So, I don't want you cuttin' him up, ya hear?"

Raymond glanced over at me. I said, "Might not be any need, Fred. Things sound pretty straight forward. I'll be headed out to Badger Creek as soon as you can sketch me a map of where this happened."

Before Fred could answer his attention was diverted to the street where an old green Pontiac was stopped. A middle-aged man and woman were looking our way. They were crass and disrespectful. The man's voice floated from the woman's open window, "Looks like O'Leary has got himself a customer."

Fred heard the man, we all did. He took a couple of steps away from the gurney and towards the street. He shouted. "Go on, get the hell outta here, you damned looky-loos."

The woman turned away and said something to the man that we couldn't quite make out and then the car moved on, but not as fast as one might expect given the situation.

Fred shook his head. "What's wrong with people these days?"

I knew that Fred's question was mostly rhetorical but I said anyway, so as to not leave it just hanging in the air, "I don't know, maybe it's the times." And then the awkwardness of where we were cried out to me as another car suddenly slowed as it went by. I caught Raymond's eye and nodded in the direction of the door. I said, "Maybe you should take Teddy inside."

Raymond looked relieved and started pulling the gurney through the door. As he did, Fred raised his left hand and jabbed his index finger at him. "Remember, no autopsy. It ain't necessary."

Raymond glanced up just as the gurney disappeared inside. For a couple of seconds his focus was fixated on Fred's bloody hands. His eyes appeared uncomfortable, like he was envisioning how Fred's hands came to look the way they did. He said, "OK, Mr. Bolander. We'll certainly try to respect your wishes."

I jumped in. "Fred, you suppose you can come over to my pickup for a minute so we can put down on paper where this happened?"

Fred started in as he trailed behind me. "Well, it's clear the hell up in the head of Badger Crik. There's a faint two-track that goes off to the east just after you cross Porphyry Crik. You go up there maybe a half mile and there's a clearing where we got some posts piled. You can't miss it."

I opened the door to my truck and took out a yellow legal pad and scribbled down what he had just told me. I studied it for a moment to see that it made sense before turning back to Fred who had been looking on. I said, "From the clearing where was it you found Teddy?"

Fred stared down at the ground for a moment like he was reconstructing in his mind where he had found Teddy's body. Finally, he began, "From the pile of posts that's furthest west you go kinda northwest for about a hundred yards and you'll run into a shallow draw there. It goes pretty much north for about two hundred yards and then it just pitches up pretty steep and ends on a little rise just short of a patch of quakies. They had that old gun tied to a tree with baling wire. It was aimed straight out to a hind quarter of lamb that was tied to their trigger rope."

"OK, hold on a second, Fred. I ain't no court stenographer so let me draw this out too."

"Hell, gimme yer pen. I'll draw it for you."

"Yeah, if you would just from the post pile." I handed my pen and tablet to Fred. As he began to draw, I could see that his knuckles on both hands were badly bruised and slightly swollen. I think he sensed that I had picked up on this but before I could ask, he offered up, "You're probably gonna run into that mutton herder out there. He's gonna tell ya that I gave him a thrashing, which I did."

"And why did you do that?" I asked, as if I didn't know.

Fred snorted. "C'mon, Andy. There's a thousand head of woolies just down the canyon from where this set gun is at.' He paused and laughed sarcastically. "It don't take Sherlock Holmes to figure that one out."

It seemed that a good amount of Fred's sadness had morphed into anger. I noted it but chose to ignore it. Nonetheless, I had to remind him of the obvious. "I know you're hurtin' Fred, but you can't be attacking people like you did. That's a pretty serious offense."

"Well then, why don't you just make my day and arrest me. You're the big shot cop. C'mon, put the bracelets on me if you're man enough."

"Fred, I know this is a bad time for you so I'm gonna let this go for now. You go on and tend to what you've got to do and I'll be in touch with you tomorrow."

Tears came to Fred's eyes. He shook his head slightly. "I'm sorry, Andy."

I looked at him, helpless to do anything other than what I was doing, delaying the inevitable. I said simply, "I know."

CHAPTER THREE

It was a little less than a thirty-minute drive to the small town of Cedarville. The highway going there had long stretches that climbed up and down gentle sage and grass covered hills. Patches of ponderosa pine broke the otherwise monotonous terrain. It was a much better road now than when I had been a deputy, some 20 years ago, living in the county's tiny one room cabin on the north edge of town. According to the state of Montana there were 23 people living here but, having been a past resident, I knew for a fact there were only 14. In my opinion, the term town had been loosely applied to Cedarville. It was a wide spot in the road at the mouth of the Gros Ventre river valley. Nonetheless, it offered the most critical staples namely food, gas, a phone and the occasional opportunity to socialize whether it be at the Antler Bar or the community church.

A little south of town, I slowed my truck to 35 mph as I went past the cemetery with its yellow grass. In a few seconds I was beyond the headstones and into the shadow of several huge cottonwood trees that towered over a dingy gray brick building with a flat roof that housed a gas station. A sign in bold black letters hung above a single garage bay door, it read: Flats Fixed Here. Out front was a Mobil gas pump. It had a large glass cylinder on top of the pump housing. On the side of this assembly was a handle that a person worked back and forth to fill the cylinder. The number of gallons it contained was printed on the glass so the customer knew how much gas he was getting. On the other side of the trees, I came to the guts of the town. To my right was a white brick building that housed the general store and on my left was the Antler Bar. Badly weathered log walls and a tattered green shingle roof seemed to betray its false front with its new coat of stain. Across the street was a newer log structure. The American flag was flying out front. This was the Lumberjack Café and post office. And then, just as I was about to leave town, I passed by the red brick school. It looked out of place in Cedarville having been built only twelve years ago. There were just two classrooms for grades one through six. The school that I had gone to had been torn down to make room for this one. On the other side of the road was the county's cabin and my old home. To look at it now brought back memories, some good and some not. On the good side it was when my wife Ellen and I had started dating and eventually got married. The things on the bad side I tried to not think about. It made me smile though to see the cabin's bright red screen door and screened window frames tucked into the walls of gray logs. Painting them red had been Ellen's idea but the screens were mine. I'd spent too many hot summer nights swatting flies to not make it better for the next guy once I became sheriff. But then I was past the cabin and the Antler Bar too and the memories they held. I sighed as I stepped down on the gas of my old Ford pickup and wound it out to almost 50 before slipping it into fourth gear and heading up the Gros Ventre river valley. County road 29 was paved now, at least for the next 30 miles it was. But this wasn't exactly true either as the county, in their perpetual state of poverty, hadn't done much maintenance on it. It seemed the potholes and frost heaves got progressively worse the further from Cedarville you went. Unfortunately, the turnoff to Badger Creek was about five miles beyond the end of the pavement. It was a nice summer day, at least weather wise it was. I had my window down with my arm out and the radio on. Ray Price was singing, *because my heart tells me stay but my pride tells me go*. The lyrics kind of temporarily cleansed my mind of all that had happened this morning and what likely awaited me up Badger Creek. I drove on through the irrigated pasture and fields of hay and grain that gave way to the sagebrush and ultimately the many timbered canyons that climbed so steeply they became bare mountain peaks. They were shades of gray and orange and even a purple of sorts. A smattering of diehard snowbanks clung to some of them as they slowly wilted under the hot August sun. Far below, stringers of trees and brush paralleled the creeks that ran from the canyons down to the valley floor and the Gros Ventre river. In a way the creeks reminded me of blood veins that emptied into an artery.

The brown wooden forest service sign marking the turnoff to Badger Creek had just come into view when Millie came over the radio.

I wrestled my mic from its metal slot on the dash. "Go ahead, Millie."

"Andy, I got a call from the hospital ER. They said Orville Stroud brought in one of his herders. I guess he's hurt pretty bad. They said Stroud told them the guy got dragged by his horse, but the ER doctor said the man's injuries don't add up to that being what happened. He thought the whole thing was kind of suspicious so he called us."

"Well, what does the herder have to say about it?"

"Nothing, he's in a coma."

I said to myself, *oh shit,* as I grimaced knowing that Fred's situation had just gotten worse. "All right, Millie. Keep this under your hat. I'm just now starting up the Badger Creek road."

"You be careful."

"I'll try. Talk to ya later."

The first mile and half of the Badger Creek road went across a sagebrush flat. It was rough and slow going which gave me time to ponder why Stroud was being devious about what had happened to his herder. I briefly considered the possibility it was because his Basque herder was here illegally and he didn't want to draw attention to him. But that thought vanished almost before it was fully formed in favor of the most likely, which was Stroud had learned that a set gun put out by his herder had killed Teddy Bolander and now he was in big trouble if this could be traced back to him. On the other hand, if the set gun couldn't be tied to the herder or Stroud, where did that leave me? I sighed heavily. In the short term, I'd most likely have to arrest Fred for assaulting the herder, ignoring the fact that most people in the valley would view what he had done as justifiable. It didn't help matters that the herder's employer, Orville Stroud, was a Californian with lots of money who had come to the valley a few years ago and began buying up ranches. Stroud Land & Cattle was now the biggest operator in the county. This was a fact that didn't sit well with more than a few people, among them was Phil Lujack, my father in law. His former employer, Milo Peterson, was one of those who had sold out to Stroud and left the country. Since I had moved my family to Fremont about ten years ago, we didn't see Ellen's parents nearly as much as when we had lived in the valley. But there didn't seem to be any way around the move as my being sheriff pretty much required that I live closer to the office. I knew, however, from our occasional visits back and forth, that Phil didn't particularly care for how Orville Stroud did things.

I was still deep in thought about how it would be viewed if I were to arrest Fred when a rooster tail of dust emerged from the trees at the mouth of Badger Creek canyon. Within a few seconds I recognized the green Dodge pickup making the dust cloud as belonging to Myron Cheevers, our local game warden. Right away I began to second guess my decision to not call him this morning and tell him about the illegal set gun but, in my defense, there just didn't seem like there was time.

Myron squeezed over to the right side of the narrow road as his truck came to a stop. He leaned out his open window and launched a stream of tobacco juice into the floury dirt below. Pulling back, he dabbed briefly at his bushy black moustache with the back of his hand. He said, in a voice as big as he was, "So, how's the county's top law dog fairin' this fine afternoon?"

I nodded. "Doin' alright, and you?"

"Well, I'm still on the right side ah the dirt."

I laughed politely. "I meant to call you this morning."

"About that Bolander kid?"

"Yeah, I guess he stumbled into a set gun just as his dog triggered it. He caught a 30-30 slug right in the chest."

Beads of sweat were running from the black hair covering Cheevers' temples. He sighed as he tilted his straw cowboy hat slightly back so as to allow cool air to reach his forehead. He said, "It's a sad damned deal. As far as I'm concerned, set guns are the work of the devil."

"I'm headed up here to where Bolander was cuttin' posts to see if I can find this gun. You're welcome to come along."

"Well, I just came from there and I couldn't find zip."

I purposely flooded my face with a question mark.

Cheevers came back. "I stopped into the store in Cedarville just after Bolander had left. Mrs. Hough filled me in on what had happened. I was by where Fred was loggin' a few days ago so I knew right off where to go, or at least I thought I knew. I found their posts, even their chainsaw and gas can, but I'll be damned if I could find any set gun."

"Fred drew me a map so maybe we'll have better luck."

"Well, hells-bells, Kimosabe, I'll follow you."

"All right," I said and then I started out slow until I could see in my rearview mirror that Cheevers had gotten turned around. I then sped up. Badger Creek canyon was more like a big basin with lots of canyons and lesser creeks than a single canyon. The country to either side of the road up the bottom of it was a mosaic of timber and sage and willow choked creeks and sometimes Quaking Aspen patches. After about 15 minutes we came to the two-track next to Porphyry Creek. To say that this was a rough road was putting it mildly as it would rattle the fillings out of your teeth but, finally, we broke out of the dense timber into the clearing where Fred had his posts piled. I got out of my truck and started towards Myron with the yellow paper in hand. It was ironic, but in that very instant a sudden peaceful feeling came over me, brought on I suppose by the smell of freshly cut pine and the silence that swallowed up the lonesome screech of a Stellers's jay flying overhead. For a brief moment, my senses rebelled against the aura of death that hung over the little meadow. They took me back to better times when I was a boy and my father was alive and we would go hunting. And then Myron slammed the door of his pickup. I turned to him and nodded towards the piles of posts. "I guess we gotta go beyond that furthest bunch of posts and head up that draw."

Myron fell in beside me. He said, looking at the tree stumps straight out from us, "Ole Bolander has been pretty busy here."

"Yeah, he's got lots ah posts to plant by his self."

Myron glanced over at me like I was being flippant, but said nothing.

I came back quick lest he think that was how I was being. I said, "It's a damned shame Fred losing his boy. His family are ranchers through and through. Now, there may not be anyone to carry that on once he's gone."

"Ain't he got any other kids?"

"Another boy, I think."

"Well, there ya go. Maybe he'll want to take over the place."

Images of my own kids flashed in my mind. It was hard for me to envision our daughter, Emma, staying in Fremont after she graduated next year. On the other hand, my son, Roy, who we had given his grandpa's middle name, would be content to stay here forever fighting fire for the forest service. Neither of them, however, wanted to go into law enforcement which suited me and their mother just fine.

We soon came to the lip of the draw that Fred had described and dropped down into it. The pine duff became heavier here, disguising the cobbly rock beneath it. Weaving in and out of Douglas fir trees, we steadily climbed. From behind me, I could hear Myron's labored breathing. He said, almost like it was a plea to take a break, "This old fat boy needs to do this more often or not at all."

I laughed and paused, looking back at him. Myron was a good ten years younger than me, but his belly mostly hid his belt buckle. I said jokingly, "Bout another half mile to go."

Myron shot back, not quite certain if I was serious, "Are you shitin' me?"

I laughed again. "No, it's less than a hundred yards if I understood Fred right."

Myron smiled and continued the friendly banter. "Well, it's a good thing. These cowboy boots might impress the girls but they ain't worth a dam for hiking."

I glanced at his pointed toe boots and their slick flat soles. I grinned, "Next time, you might wanna leave yer dancin' slippers home."

In a few minutes we topped out at the head of the draw and just like Fred had said, there was a little patch of quaking aspen. More importantly though was a dark, almost black, blood stain not five feet in front of us. It was good sized suggesting that Teddy had lost a lot of blood, probably in a hurry. The grass was matted down where he had lain and in the crusted blood were several dog tracks. Between where we were standing and where the aspens got thick it was about 15 or 20 yards of grass and wildflowers, nothing to intercept a bullet.

Myron sighed heavily. "What are the odds that kid would come along to just this spot at the very time that gun goes off?"

I shook my head, "Good enough, I guess." I looked over at the aspen trees to where the gun would have been aligned with the blood on the ground and began walking. It was a gentle incline. I stopped at the edge of the trees. After a few seconds of searching the most obvious with my eyes, I said, "I ain't seein' any gun."

"Me neither," said Myron.

I turned and looked back at the blood stain. I said, "We're straight out from where Teddy was. That gun has got to be right here somewhere."

Myron stood with his hands on his hips looking into the trees. He said, "Well, you gotta remember this thing was set to kill anything that eats sheep, but most likely a bear. It could be that it was situated to our left or right and aimed to shoot back at an angle across this little opening."

I was about to agree with Myron when I caught sight of what looked like a fresh cut on a big tree about ten feet back into the thicket. Staring hard at the spot, I started toward it. When I was within a couple of feet of the tree I stopped and dropped to my knees. The thin slice was about two feet above the ground or the height of a bear's face when on all four legs. It went half way around the tree and ended. For an aspen, the tree was big, maybe 12 to 14 inches in diameter where the slice marks were.

"Whaddaya thinkin'?" asked Myron who was standing behind me.

"Well, it kinda looks like maybe somebody has wrapped baling wire to this tree real tight cuz it cut the bark."

Myron knelt down across from me. "Yeah, like the wire cut into the bark on that side of the tree but not this side because that's where the gun was and it was probably tied to the barrel and the stock."

"That makes sense but if Fred saw this gun here early this morning and it's now mid- afternoon and it's gone, that says to me somebody knew almost right away that their gun had killed the wrong thing."

Myron chimed in before I could finish my thought. "I suspect you're right. They musta been close by because they were Johnny-on-the-spot takin' this thing down."

And then through the tall grass I caught a glimpse of something that didn't look right protruding from a smaller tree a few feet beyond the big tree with the wire slice. I crawled over to it on my hands and knees and parted the grass. I instantly called out to Myron, "Got a rusty staple sticking outta this tree."

Myron moved over to where he could see the staple. He snorted, "Well, there you have it just bigger 'n shit, some old boy has had a set gun here. He ran a string from the trigger back through this staple and then back out to a piece of meat in front of the gun. Old mister bear comes along and says why here's a free lunch and picks it up in his paws or mouth and tries to back away even an inch and boom, the gun goes off."

"I guess Teddy's dog must have come at the meat from the side and started pulling. I saw his nose. It wasn't pretty."

Myron shook his head. "Lucky for the dog and none at all for the kid."

"Well, I guess when God was dishing out bad luck to the Bolander family today, he gave Fred an extra helping."

Myron scoffed. "That's for damned sure." He paused and looked at me like there was more to what I had to say, which there was.

I came back. "When Fred headed outta here with his boy layin' dead in the back of his truck he ran into one of Orville Stroud's sheepherders down the canyon. I guess they got into it and Fred beat him pretty bad."

"Who threw the first punch?"

"Sounds like Fred did. The herder is in a coma."

Myron tossed his head to the side. "Ho-lee shit. When it rains it pours, don't it?"

I nodded. "It sure has on Fred."

Out of the blue, Myron shot back, "You gonna arrest him for assault?"

Myron's question didn't come as a surprise. I had been trying ever since the funeral home to ignore the prospect of having to do that. Even after Millie called with the herder's condition, I was still hopeful that somehow arresting Fred could be avoided, but now here was Myron slapping me in the face with it.

He probed my silence. "I sure don't envy you. If you arrest Fred, there'll be folks that'll drop ya from their Christmas card list and if ya don't, well hell, I don't know if you could get away with that."

"I know, there'll be some people that say the herder had it coming. I'd tend to agree with them if he put the set gun out, but right now we don't have a gun so I guess that leaves Fred in a bad spot."

Myron came back, the both of us still on our knees there in the tall grass beneath the aspens, "Well, I'll bet you a dollar to a pickled dog turd that if that herder didn't put out this gun then Orville Stroud or one of his hands did."

I shook my head. "I've no doubt you're right."

Myron went silent, acting as if he was preoccupied with fishing his foil pouch of Beechnut chewing tobacco out of his hip pocket. He brought it forward, opened it, pulled out a good-sized pinch and put it in his mouth between his cheek and gum without looking at me. He continued to let the silence grow between us save for a gust of wind that rattled the leaves of the trees and a raven cawing off in the distance. And then he said, in what I suppose was his best attempt to sound innocent in what he was suggesting, "You know, I betcha there's probably someone in the valley that's got the skookum on who put this gun out here."

I laughed in a tone just one notch down from being sarcastic and said, "Myron, I was hopin' to not involve Phil in this."

Myron turned his head to the side and spit, "Well, he does work for Stroud."

I ignored Myron's last statement like I was done talking about my father-in-law, because I was, and reached into my shirt pocket for my little Kodak instamatic camera. I said, "I believe I'll get some pictures of all this and then I figure I'll head for the barn."

Myron gave me an awkward look for a few seconds before saying, "Sounds good to me but just know that I'll be wantin' to have a come to Jesus talk with whoever rigged this thing up."

I said, while looking through the little window on my camera at the staple, "I know, Myron. I'll share anything I find out with you."

"You wanna go talk to Stroud today?" asked Myron just before pausing to spit onto the trunk of an aspen off to his left. "You know me, I ain't shy about such things."

Tracking Stroud down and confronting him with his version of how his herder came to be in the hospital was next on my list of things to do, but I wasn't certain if I wanted Myron along. He'd been known to get a little heavy handed with people who had acquired a reputation for having things their way. Orville Stroud fell into that category. This past winter he shot three elk that had gotten into one of his haystacks and then called the game department and told them to *come get their damned elk off his land.* Last I heard Stroud had never been charged with anything, but it was a permanent burr under Myron's saddle. I said, "My intention is to swing by the hospital when I get to town. With his herder being so bad off I figure Stroud may still be there."

Myron came back quick. "Sounds good to me."

I allowed a feeble but wry smile to come to my face. I said, "I know Stroud isn't one of your favorite people so –"

Myron cut me off. "Well, do you like the sonovabitch?"

I hesitated but then said, "No, but I believe I can hold my temper while I talk to him."

"I can too unless he gets smart with me."

"All right, you've got to remember that cuz we don't want to give him cause to make a complaint against us."

Myron grinned. "Don't worry, I'll put on my best boy scout manners. It'll make ya proud." And then he laughed.

After taking a bunch of pictures of the crime scene we took our leave of it and headed for town. On the way we drove by the old Peterson place. The house had been torn down at the insistence of Mrs. Stroud and replaced with a big fancy new log house that resembled a lodge, more than somebody's home. My father-in-law told me the place even had a swimming pool in the back yard but few people had ever seen it since the yard was enclosed in a six-foot high cedar board fence. From the road a white Cadillac was visible in the garage but Stroud's pickup, which I'd been told just last Sunday when my in-laws came to dinner, was a brand spanking new 1965 blue four-wheel drive Chevy, was nowhere to be seen. I had heard at length how much it likely cost and how '*uppity*' people thought Stroud's wife was for tearing down what had been the nicest house in the valley just because it was old. To quote my father in law, *I guess that just make's the rest of us white hillbilly trash*. But, while Phil would talk this way at Sunday dinner, he seldom ever was critical of Stroud to anybody out in the Gros Ventre valley. He knew better and so did I. When I had lived there, gossiping about your neighbor was recreation to a lot of people. A person never knew where what was said while leaning on an irrigation shovel or over the hood of a pickup might end up. And, if you were dumb enough to bare your soul at the Antler Bar it was a good bet that it would soon be common knowledge in the valley. Given all this, it made my decision to drive right on by my in-laws' place, which Stroud owned, and keep as a last resort asking Phil what he might know about Stroud putting out a set gun.

It was 5:40 P.M. as I rolled slowly through Cedarville with Myron close behind. There were a couple of pickups in front of the Lumberjack Café and an old black Hudson nosed in at the Antler Bar. A brown dog lay in the sliver of shade afforded by its rear bumper. The big hill to the west of town, which was dotted with ponderosa pine in a sea of sagebrush, was in the early stages of casting a shadow. Ralph Hough, a middle-aged guy from Billings who had bought the store five years ago was out front sweeping the concrete porch. He looked up at me and then Myron but he did not wave, he just stared until we were out of sight.

The hospital in Fremont was situated on the side of a hill overlooking the town. It was a one story, cream-colored brick building that until about ten years ago, didn't exist. The street leading up to it snaked its way through a small enclave of nice houses with well-kept lawns and flower beds and big pine trees. It was an area commonly referred to by the town's people as where the rich folks lived. Coming out of the last curve the street became even steeper before it emptied into the hospital parking lot. There were spaces for maybe a dozen cars with about half of these already taken. One of the vehicles was a brand spanking new blue Chevy pickup. Myron and I parked next to it. I paused at the back of the pickup and looked in. There were 25 or 30 white blocks of salt, a couple of empty gunny sacks, a tow chain and a shovel, but nothing that was incriminating.

Myron came along side of me. "Hell, it still smells new."

I glanced over at him and grinned, "In my lifetime that's something I've never gotten very well acquainted with."

"Well, me neither. This was just a lucky guess."

We were both laughing, not a belly-buster but just an easy feel-good moment when beyond us towards the hospital door an unfriendly voice called out, "You boys find something that interests you in my pickup?"

I looked in the direction of the voice as did Myron. Under his breath he mumbled, "Well, there's that sonovabitch now."

I glanced at Myron and frowned before calling out to Stroud who was walking towards us, "I got a call about one of your herders being hurt."

Stroud was a medium sized man with short brown hair who appeared to be about my age. His clean-shaven face feigned surprise as he continued walking. When he was within conversation distance he stopped and looked at me as if Myron was non-existent, he said, "I don't see how my herder's horse dragging him is cause for the law to be involved. Did that damned doctor call you? I told him he was full of shit when he started spoutin' off about his suspicions and-"

"Fred Bolander told me what happened."

Stroud's face became pale and his green slightly blood-shot eyes looked away nervously as he frantically pondered if he should go on with the lie. He snorted, "Well, that dumbass. I was just trying to save everybody some grief."

"How's that?"

"My man didn't go through the proper channels getting here but Bolander assaulted him. I figured if I don't report the assault no one needs to report Felipe being illegal."

I shook my head slightly. "Didn't you wonder why Bolander attacked your herder?"

Fear instantly surfaced in Stroud's eyes. He came back in an angry tone, "Oh, he had some bullshit idea that Felipe had put out a set gun that killed his boy."

I looked hard at Stroud. "Well, did he?"

"Hell no. I'm still fightin' with the game department over that elk deal last winter. You think I want to stir up more trouble with them?"

Myron broke his silence. "I don't think that matters to you."

Stroud glanced at Myron and then back at me. "You need to tell your fish cop buddy here that one call from me to the governor and he'll be pumping gas somewhere."

Myron snorted. "Why you worthless little turd I-"

I stepped in front of Myron and blocked his view of Stroud, I whispered, "Boy scout manners, remember?"

For a brief moment, he stared beyond me. Over my shoulder I could hear Stroud laugh sarcastically. "Go ahead, start something. See where that gets you."

I wheeled around to face Stroud. "You might want to rein in the smart mouth, Mr. Stroud, cuz if there's anybody here on thin ice it's you." I scoffed, "Let's just cut the crap. Any third party that was to come upon what happened up Badger Creek this morning would come to the same conclusion as Fred Bolander and, chances are, they'd do just what he did. So, why don't you come clean about this?"

Anger replaced the fear in Stroud's face. He began to slowly shake his head while taking a deep breath. He held this a second or two before noisily exhaling as if he was trying to control his rage. He said, emphatically, "If I was responsible for putting that set gun out I'd fess up, but I didn't do it."

Myron jumped in. "Why would anybody else do it?"

"Hell, I don't know. Maybe they're just a poacher or maybe they want to sell the hide or claws to a tourist. Or maybe they want to sell bear parts to the Chinese. I've heard they use gallbladders to make aphrodisiacs." Stroud paused and looked straight at me. "I didn't do this but I'll tell ya what, since you boys have decided to bust open this hornet's nest, I'm filing a complaint against Bolander. You go arrest him for assaulting my herder. And while you're at it, you can tell him I'm gonna send the hospital bill to him. Yeah, you tell him that. So, now I'd appreciate it if you two would step away from my truck so I can go on home."

As much as I felt Stroud was responsible for Teddy's death, I didn't have a shred of solid proof to base an arrest on. Myron and I stepped back to let Stroud by. He was smug in his victory as he got in his pickup and drove off. His taillights had barely disappeared around the curve leaving the parking lot when Myron asked, "You gonna arrest Bolander?"

I said, "Not tonight I'm not. The man's got enough on his plate for one day." I started toward my truck pausing at the door to look over at Myron. "Fred knows I'll be coming for him, but I ain't gonna do that until he's buried his son."

Stroud's departure allowed the hostility to drain from Myron's face. He was back to his usual self. "Did ya hear that?"

"Hear what?"

"It's calling to me."

"What the hell are you talking about?"

Myron broke into a laugh. "A chicken fried steak down at the Coffee Cup."

I grinned and gave him a dismissive wave as I climbed into my truck and headed down the hill.

From the hospital to where I lived at the edge of town was about a ten-minute drive. It required that I go past the grain elevator, over the train tracks, through Fremont's only traffic light and right on down main street with its assorted businesses. Among these were three bars, two drug stores, two cafes, a clothing store, bank, movie theater, two gas stations, two doctor's offices, a Ford dealership and lastly, where things began to peter out, Brewer's Drive-In. My daughter, Emma, had been working there this summer. Next week, when school starts, she would be cutting back to a couple of hours each day after school and six hours on Saturdays. As I went by I spotted her long black hair. She was standing with a tray of food next to a car's open window. Her back was to the street. I thought of honking but the image of her turning and spilling the tray came to mind, so I did not. After another mile of scattered houses and trailers, storage sheds, corrals, and parked cars that hadn't run in a long time, I came to Yellow Dog Road and turned. About a quarter mile up ahead was our home, or at least it was as long as we continued to make the payments to the Stockman's Bank for the next twelve years and three months. It was a dark red clapboard house with white wood trim and rust colored tarpaper shingles. A big maple tree grew from the center of the lawn out front but, what caught a person's eye were the flowers. They were my wife Ellen's passion. There were red and yellow roses, white daisies, big blue lupines, red geraniums and hollyhocks of all colors that grew above the top rail of the four and half-foot tall chicken wire fence that we'd built to keep Bella, our black Lab, from wandering. Through the open garage door, I could see our brown '58 Chevy Impala. The sight of it right away caused a good feeling within me as I knew Ellen had made it safely home from Bozeman. I parked in the driveway, somewhat surprised that Bella wasn't waiting for me in the front yard and went in through the garage which opened into the utility room. After hanging my straw cowboy hat and gun belt on a peg next to the washer, I went into the kitchen. Everything was quiet until I heard Bella start barking from what sounded like the patio, followed by, "We're out here."

I went through the living room and slid the screen door back and stepped outside. Bella was first to greet me with lots of tail wagging and prancing around. Ellen got up from her lawn chair and leaned past Bella to give me a kiss. "How was your day?"

Today had not been good. None of the days where I had to deal with somebody dying were good but, as much as possible, I tried to keep the emotional baggage that went with those deaths to myself. I said, "Did you talk to Millie?"

"No, but I heard about the Bolander boy. That's just awful. I feel so bad for Fred and Norma."

"You just got into town. Where'd you hear about this?"

"I stopped for gas at the Conoco on my way home. That Collins boy works there. He seemed to know all about it."

I frowned and shook my head. "What else did he know?"

"He knew that Fred beat up a sheepherder and that you're probably gonna throw him in jail."

"Well, unless he was a fly on the wall at O'Leary's funeral home, I doubt he could've learned about this any other way."

A sudden awareness came to Ellen's dark eyes. "There was a black hearse parked in the garage bay. They must've been working on it."

I sighed, "Juicy gossip travels fast, I guess."

Ellen's demeanor suddenly changed like she'd lost interest in the grief of the Bolander family. She picked up an unopened letter laying on the end table next to her chair and held it up to me. "This came for Roy today."

I took the letter and looked at the return address. Anger and fear instantly boiled up within me. I frowned and handed it back to her. I said, "I'm gonna get a beer, you want one?"

Ellen tossed the letter on the end table and nodded towards a big jar of sun tea sitting on the corner of the patio. "I guess we'll have that later."

"Yeah, Roy likes tea when it's this hot."

I went inside and got a couple of Budweisers from the fridge. When I returned Ellen was looking at the outside of the letter again like maybe if she looked at it long enough she would see it wasn't addressed to Roy, and that the mailman had made a mistake. I handed her a beer and sat down in the chair next to hers'. She said, "Maybe they're just changing his classification. Remember, I told you that I saw Irma Hollis at the IGA a couple of weeks ago. I made it a point to tell her that Roy had submitted all of his paperwork so he could go to school in Bozeman this fall."

I took a long drink of my beer. The carbonation welled up in my throat almost causing my eyes to water but the beer's coldness felt good. I said, "You suppose you're the only mother with a draft age son that corners Irma in the grocery store to plead her case so she'll run home and tell Bill?"

"It wasn't like that."

"I know. I'm tempted every time I see Bill to let him know what a good kid Roy is and that he's got a lot to live for, but I don't."

Ellen gave me a surprised look but then something caused her to back away from it. Maybe it was the image of Willie Elkins' funeral procession going slowly down Fremont's Main Street not two months ago. Cars pulled over. People stopped on the sidewalk and watched quietly as Willie rolled by. He had tripped a booby trap in Vietnam that had blown his legs off from the knees down. He bled out before they could get him to a hospital and, he was a good kid too.

I said, "I don't envy Bill Hollis being on the draft board. It's a thankless job. Why, you think he doesn't want to slip out the side door if he was to run into Willie Elkins' father at the CO-OP or some such. I bet-"

Ellen cut in, "All right, Andy, you've made your point."

I came back quick, as it had flashed in my mind how I was being, "I'm sorry, Honey. I just-"

"I know, I know, but I think it's different for a mother. Last week Harriet Elkins dropped by the office to pay their grazing fees. She looked sad. Her eyes had dark circles beneath them. She looked like she could cry."

I sighed and shook my head. "I imagine she's had more than her share of doing that."

Bella, who had been laying in the grass at the edge of the patio, suddenly jumped up and started running around the side of the house, barking as she went.

"Roy must be coming up the road," said Ellen.

I laughed. "I swear that dog can hear Roy coming before he leaves the city limits."

And then the sadness that Ellen had just talked about seemed to overtake her. She said, "Bella is really going to miss Roy."

"He ain't gone yet. Maybe he won't even go."

The rumble of Roy's '55 Chevy now became audible to us, getting louder and louder until it was in front of the house and abruptly shut off, but not before he raced the engine a couple of times to listen to the car's loud pipes back down, music to a 19 year-old boy's ears. Moments later, Bella came back panting with her tail wagging. She pressed her nose next to the screen door. Inside, the door to the garage slammed shut, followed by, "I'm home."

Ellen shouted, "Get yourself a glass of ice. There's fresh tea out here."

"OK, be right there."

In a way I felt guilty just sitting there knowing that a short time from now my son's world would be, so to speak, turned upside down and there wasn't a thing I could do about it. The mood in the air, at least where Ellen and I were, reminded me of last winter when we had to tell the kids that their great grandpa had died. After the war, he and Grandma Tanaka had been released from the Heart Mountain internment camp. They settled and started their lives down in Casper, Wyoming where they made a modest living running their own restaurant. During the summer, the kids enjoyed spending time with their grandparents. Roy especially liked to go there because he and his great grandpa went fishing a lot.

Roy slid the screen door open. Bella was first to greet him. "Oh, what a silly dog you are," he said in an excited voice as he ruffled her ears. "You're just beside yourself, aren't you?" And then he went over to the gallon jar that used to hold pickles and un-screwed the lid. Over his shoulder, he said, "You want me to take the tea bags out?"

"Yes, that would be good," said Ellen.

Roy poured his tea and moved to the chair across from me and sat down, He said, "Boy, I tell you what I'm ready for fall. We were clearing trail today up on Otter Creek and I liked to have melted down."

In that instant I imagined Roy in Vietnam and wondered how would he ever deal with the intense heat and humidity there. I caught his eye and said, in a tone that was maybe too serious, "You got a letter today."

Roy laughed but then said, "Well, that doesn't sound good. Hmm, what could it be? It's too early for Santa Claus to turn down my wish list." And then he laughed again, but nervously, as he leaned over to take the letter from his mother's outstretched hand.

"Maybe it's a reclassification," said Ellen hopefully. "You wrote them didn't you and told them you were going to college this fall?"

"I did, probably a month ago."

I threw in, as if more words to the contrary could change what was in the letter, "Yeah, I betcha that's it. They're changing you from a 1A to a 1SH or whatever it was you said that was."

Roy had barely opened the letter when the hope vanished from his face. He read aloud, in a mocking tone, "Greetings: You are hereby ordered for induction into the Armed Forces of the United States, and to report at…" His voice trailed off as he read on before suddenly shrieking, "Shit, they want me to report to the U.S. Post Office in Livingston at 6:30 A.M. on the 20th of August."

"The 20th," said Ellen disbelievingly. "Why that's." she paused counting calendar days in her head, "that's next Tuesday. They can't do that. You'll have to quit your job with the forest service, and school? I don't know if you need to notify them since you've been accepted for this fall." And then she looked at me with some desperation in her eyes like she didn't know this was coming. "Can they do this, Andy? Maybe you should call Bill Hollis."

I shrugged and shook my head. "I don't think there's much we can do."

Ellen looked at Roy. "Well, isn't your knee bad from that time you hurt it playing football? Maybe you won't pass the physical."

Roy laughed trying to be brave and indifferent to what was happening to him. "Mom. I'm fighting fires and doing trail maintenance. Some days I hike six or seven miles in the mountains. I doubt any doctor is gonna say my knee isn't good enough for the Army."

Relentless, Ellen came back. "Well, you know that Cooper boy. His mother told me he went and joined the Air Force when he got his draft notice and now he's stationed over at Spokane."

"Yeah, well I know Doug Cooper and he doesn't like it and he's got four years to do."

Ellen leaned forward in her chair and looked intently at Roy. She said in a sharp tone like that's what was necessary for him to understand the importance of what she was about to say, "Well, most likely he'll be alive at the end of those four years."

Fear, with a twist of anger, surfaced in Roy's face. "Gee, thanks for pointing that out, Mom."

Tears immediately came to Ellen's eyes as she sank back in her chair. I said, "Roy, your mom is just afraid for you. We both are.".

Roy did not back away from his anger. He said, sarcastically, "Well, I guess that makes three of us that are afraid for me going to Vietnam."

"If that's the case, why not take your mother's advice?"

"Dad, I've been thinking a lot about this. I like my life the way it is. I don't want to go do something else, especially when I really don't see the need for it, but I don't really have a choice. I know a guy who was drafted, went into the Army and after his training and a year in Vietnam he was discharged after 18 months. And he said it wasn't that bad."

I sighed. "I guess for some guys it works out ok, but your mother and I tend to look at what happened to Willie Elkins."

"Or that Hawkins boy that works at the Husky station," said Ellen. "The war changed him. Before he went in the Army, he was always chipper and made jokes and now when I go there, he pumps my gas and barely says a word."

"At least he came back alive," said Roy.

"So did your Uncle Melvin," said Ellen, as if she had just declared checkmate.

I looked at Ellen. Her right eye had dislodged a single tear that was working its way down her cheek. The mention of her brother's name had caused her and Roy to go silent. Years ago, during WWII Melvin had been discharged from the Army Air Corps due to emotional distress. He was akin to another "Hawkins boy" in the way he acted, except he'd gone up into the mountains above the Gros Ventre river and stuck a .38 in his mouth and pulled the trigger. Ellen's other brother was in the Marines. He was buried on Okinawa. So, she knew firsthand about the heartache war could cause. These were facts that Roy was aware of, he said, "There's no need to cry, Mom. I'll talk to the Air Force recruiter."

Ellen's expression brightened. "Maybe you could get stationed at that base they've got up at Great Falls. How good would that be?"

"That'd be real good, Mom."

"We could come see you on weekends or you could come down here. That wouldn't be bad, don't you think?"

Roy took a drink of his ice tea and then parroted back to his mother, "No, that wouldn't be bad, Mom."

Ellen, who could read Roy as well as I could allowed herself to indulge in the fantasy that he really would talk to the Air Force recruiter.

CHAPTER FOUR

I'd already had two cups of coffee at home with my break-fast, but when I was in the office force of habit associated with doing paperwork caused me to have a third. I was mid-pour when the phone rang at Millie's desk, followed by, "I'll let you talk to the Sheriff."

I made eye contact with Millie thereby saving her the trouble of hollering at me and went to my desk. I answered my phone while still standing, "Sheriff Yarnell, how can I help you?"

"This is Doctor Buckley up at the hospital."

"Oh, yes, how are you?"

"I'm doing well, thank-you. The reason I'm calling is I need to get in touch with Orville Stroud. His employee that he brought in yesterday died during the night."

The doctor's words caught me by surprise. I blurted out, "He died?"

"Yes, Mr. Arriola's head injuries were fairly severe. He had a fractured skull, broken jaw, broken nose and a number of teeth that had been knocked out. This was no horse-riding accident, Sheriff. Somebody gave him a good beating."

"I know."

"You do?"

"Yes."

There was a slightly awkward pause on the doctor's end while he considered, I supposed, asking for details, but he said, "Mr. Stroud indicated he would be back this morning. Arrangements will need to be made."

My mind leaped ahead to the shitstorm of trouble that this was going to create for the Bolander family. It caused me to sigh heavily into the phone before coming back to the issue at hand, "I'll notify the coroner. He'll be up to get the body."

Buckley then offered, "It's despicable what happened to Mr. Arriola. I think Mr. Stroud knows far more about this than he's telling."

"I'm sure it'll all come out in the end. It's hard to keep secrets in a small community."

And then, as if he was going to test my theory about secrets, he asked, "Have you got any idea who might have done this?"

I'm not a practiced liar, so I said, "Nothing that I can share."

"So, you do have a suspect?"

I thought, *hell, if he goes by the Conoco for gas he'll know as much as I do*, but I said, "I can't really say."

"All right, I understand. I guess we can expect the coroner sometime this morning?"

The image of O'Leary driving his hearse up to the hospital caused a wry smile to come to my face. *That'll be like the town crier reporting the news if I don't say something*. I said into the phone, "You can, I'll call him as soon as we're done here."

"All right, thank-you."

I hung up the phone and immediately began thumbing through my rolodex for the number to O' Leary's funeral home. I figured, since Raymond had tangible work to do, he would be there and not at his part-time job at the CO-OP. After about a half-dozen rings, he answered, a little out of breath. "O'Leary's funeral home."

"Raymond, this is Sheriff Yarnell."

"Oh yes, how are you?"

"Well, I'm little on the cranky side this morning."

"Why is that?"

"Well, it seems the folks down at the Conoco are privy to most everything about Teddy Bolander and Stroud's sheep-herder and they've even got it on good authority, apparently, that Fred's arrest is imminent. You wouldn't happen to know anything about this, would you?"

There was absolute silence on the other end. For a second or two I thought Raymond had hung up, but then he said like a scolded schoolboy, "I'm sorry Sheriff. I didn't think it would matter."

"It does if Fred, or somebody from his family, first learns that he's going to be arrested from a kid pumping gas at the Conoco, or by now it might be the grocery store clerk, or the bartender at the Lariat, or hell who knows where. From now on, you need to keep these things to yourself."

"Yes Sir, I will. I'm sorry. I don't know what I was thinking."

Although there was truth in what I'd just told Raymond I felt bad for coming down on him, especially now that the herder had died. It was inevitable that I would have to arrest Fred. But I'd been hoping to delay that for a few days. I said, "What's done is done, Raymond. We need to put this behind us. Moving on, though, you need to go up to the hospital and pick up that herder's body. He died last night."

Raymond hesitated and then he said, surprisingly, "I guess that beating he got was pretty bad."

I allowed Raymond his little dig and said simply, "You need to be sure that it was his injuries and not some underlying health issue that killed him, even if we have to send him to the state's lab in Helena."

"All right, Sheriff, I'll get right on it."

I thought to apologize for being gruff with him, but I did not, I said only, "Thanks, Raymond." And then I hung up. I sat there pretending to be reading something on my desk as I pondered the situation with Fred. I had sufficient grounds to arrest him. He'd confessed to me that he'd beaten the herder and now the herder was dead. I told myself that if his son hadn't been killed I would've arrested him yesterday, but there was no denying the fact that Teddy was lying on a stainless-steel table with a sheet over him, waiting for his folks to come say how the service was to go. And then, in my mind's eye, I saw myself showing up and adding to their grief. Abruptly, I pushed my chair back and stood up. Millie was looking at me almost like I was acting peculiar. I glanced at her, and then the full cup of coffee on my desk, and said, "I'm going out to the Gros Ventre and poke around a bit. See what I can find out about that set gun."

Millie came back. "Well, be careful. You know some of them people out there ain't wired quite right."

I smiled as I took my hat off the peg on the wall behind my desk. "See ya this afternoon."

It was about five past nine when the Cedarville cemetery came into view. I let off the gas of my pickup and shifted down to third gear. The town appeared dead, not that it was ever real lively but this morning there was only one vehicle in sight that might be associated with a patron of some sort. It was an old red '49 Studebaker pickup in front of the Lumberjack Café. I steered off the road and parked next to it. A gray and white sheep dog with blue eyes was sitting in the bed of the truck. Next to it was a canvas dam that was wound around a ten-foot pole that stuck out a good four feet past the top of the tailgate. The handle of an irrigating shovel also extended, maybe a foot, beyond the side of the bed just behind the cab on the driver's side. I held my hand out to the dog who had got up to greet me. He gave me a couple of licks and I gave him a couple of pets.

"Well, I see you met Buster," said a loud voice off to my right as I stepped inside the café.

I looked in the direction of the voice. An old, frail looking man was sitting at a table near the window. He had on hip boots, the tops of which had been rolled down to his ankles and then back up creating a six-inch cuff. His muddy Levis were exposed from the knees up and his long-sleeved blue denim shirt that was badly faded had a hole in the left elbow. Beneath the bill of his greasy John Deere baseball cap I could see that his dark eyes were staring at me. I said, "Yeah, I did. He looks like a good dog." And then I looked away from the old man and started towards a stool at the counter.

"Bonnie, get that man a cup of coffee on me."

I paused and glanced over at the stranger. "I appreciate it but that ain't necessary."

"Any friend of Buster's is deserving of something. Hell, it's only a dime."

From the corner of my eye, I could see that Bonnie was pouring me a cup of coffee, regardless of who paid for it. Normally, I tried to avoid the appearance of getting anything for free simply because I was the sheriff. In this case, however, I figured since it was due to being friends with Buster, it might be ok. I said to the man, "Thank you. I'm much obliged." As I reached for the heavy cream-colored mug, Bonnie's thick red lips had formed into a weak smile. She whispered, "You ain't done yet."

From behind me, the old man called out, "Me an' Buster get de-flea-ed on a regular basis so yer safe to pull up a chair if ya like"

I'd intended to pick Bonnie's brain as I knew she over-heard a lot of talk every day. But the old man's expression was hopeful and I was indebted to him so I took my coffee and headed for his little table. When I was just about there, he stood up like my arrival was deserving of it and stuck out his hand. "Name's George Morgan."

I could feel the bones in his hand and his grip was not strong. I said, with extra sincerity in my voice, "Andy Yarnell, pleased to meet ya."

We sat down, strangers up until about a minute ago. George said, "Yes sir, that Buster is a good dog. Got 'im when he was just a pup from this Bassco fella."

"Buster ah sheep dog?"

George scoffed. "Oh, hell no. Mutton will never cross my lips."

I laughed and then took a drink of my coffee. "I take it you're not a sheep man."

"Nope, as far as I'm concerned the bears can eat 'em all."

My polite interest in our conversation suddenly picked up. I said, "So, do the bears give the ranchers much trouble out here?"

"Oh, some. This fella that I got Buster from works for that big shot Californian that came in here a few years ago. Now, he could tell ya about the bears, but I don't think you'll get him to talk about it."

"What's your friend's name?"

George paused and rubbed the stubble of white whiskers on his chin, like maybe he'd already said something that he shouldn't have. Finally, he said, "This ain't gonna git this guy in trouble is it?"

"I don't know, George. There's laws against killin' bears. If he's broke one of 'em, he might be."

"Well, I don't think he's done anything that his boss didn't tell him to do. What it comes down to is he kills bears or he gets fired."

I sensed that George didn't like the idea of killing bears either, so I didn't press him on the matter. I said, "Sounds like your friend is in a tough spot."

For a few seconds George stayed quiet, glancing over at Bonnie who was sitting at a card table to the left of the end of the counter. At this time of day during the winter the table would be occupied by ranchers, done with their morning feeding, playing pitch. But now, Bonnie had the Billings Gazette spread out on it. George leaned toward me and lowered his voice, "You know what's a real pisser?"

I came back with the obvious, "No, what?"

"My friend used this perfectly good rifle to set a trap for the bears. Just tied it to a tree and left it out in the woods. Can you believe that shit? A perfectly good gun just lettin' it rust away like that."

My heart rate suddenly kicked up beyond what the Lumberjack's strong coffee had already elevated it to. I said, "How is it you know this?"

"Well, about a year ago this old Indian by the name of Tony Beard died. He lived about a mile north of town along the river in an old log cabin. Well, long story short is his sister, I think she lives over on the Cheyenne Reservation, came to settle his affairs. They sold all of his stuff at auction. One of the things he had that I wanted real bad was an old Winchester 45-70."

Given George's small size, I couldn't help but blurt out, "Wow, that's a real cannon."

George grinned. "It'd be a helluva elk gun."

"I don't suppose a bear would run away from it either."

"No, and that's what that damned Stroud ended up doing with it. He outbid everybody, me included, for that gun and then not too long after that I see my Bassco friend has it hanging in the gun rack of his pickup. I commented on it and he tells me that Stroud didn't like it because it kicked too much so he gives it to Joe and tells him to use it on the bears."

"Meaning to shoot a bear if he saw it or something else?"

George momentarily scrunched his face up like, *ain't you been listening*? And then he said, his voice more emphatic, "A set gun."

"This Joe fella, you wouldn't happen to know where he put this gun would ya?"

George shook his head. "No, he didn't say but he did tell me that he's been gettin' lots ah bears. Said he's got nine so far this summer."

I reached for my coffee and took a drink hoping to disguise my anger. Lowering the cup, I went on like what he'd said was no big deal, "Well, I guess Stroud's sheep will sleep better at night because of it."

George snorted. "I reckon they will but tell me, do you personally know anybody that eats lamb chops? Do ya? I don't, other than Stroud's Basscos."

"This Joe guy, you know his last name?"

For a second George's eyes hinted that I had tricked him but then, after glancing over at Bonnie who was still deep into the Gazette, he whispered, "Garmendia."

I thought to ask him how that was spelled but I figured my guess would be as good as his so I just repeated it. "Garmendia."

"Yeah, he runs the sheep side ah things for Stroud and old Phil Lujack runs the cattle side and all the farming, at least that's my take on it."

I'd always viewed Phil as the foreman of the entire ranch, but given the current trouble on the sheep side I liked George's version of things better. I said, still trying to act only casually interested, "So, I take it your friend Joe lives up on the Stroud place?"

George nodded and then took a noisy slurp of his coffee before adding, "He lives in a little white house south of Stroud's mansion."

I was about to ask him if Joe had ever mentioned anything about being in Badger Creek recently when the door behind me opened. A middle-aged man wearing a straw cowboy hat walked in. I looked over to see that he was taking note of George and I. A worried look came to George's face. In the next instant, he drained his coffee cup and pushed back his chair. He said, as he dug into his pants pocket for money,

"Well Sheriff, I'll be seein' ya. I got water to change." And with that he dropped a quarter on the table and walked out.

Through the window, I watched George's labored walk to his pickup. He paused to pet Buster and then he got in and drove away. I wondered how his talking to me would be spun in the valley's rumor mill. In time everything that happened up Badger Creek would come out. There'd likely be people going to jail and there'd be those that agreed with that and, on the other side of the fence, those that didn't. There'd be those that'd say, *it was his daddy-n-law that spilled the beans on Joe*, and then there'd be a few that might have heard about me and George having coffee together. I sighed and got up from the table. "Be seein' ya, Bonnie."

"All right, Sheriff, you have yourself a good day."

I was a couple of miles north of Cedarville, still on the paved part of CR29, when I saw way hell and gone up ahead of me a suspicious looking green dot coming my way. At this point on 29 it is as straight as the proverbial arrow. A person's view of anything on it is not obstructed for close to three miles. However, in another 20 seconds I had sufficiently closed the gap with the green dot to where I could see that it was my father-in-law. Shortly, we rolled to a stop next to one another. Pleasantries or banter as we usually did were not in order. It was obvious that he knew. I said, "I take it you've talked to Stroud."

Phil snorted. "Oh, yeah. He gave me my marchin' orders last night."

"And those were?"

"I don't know a thing. I'm just dumber 'n a box a rocks about all this."

"Are you?"

Phil removed his sweat stained Stetson and ran his fingers through his mostly gray hair as if thinking before putting his hat back on. He looked at me and said, "I'm about 75 percent ignorant on this subject. I overheard a couple of the guys talkin' about Joe's big gun in the woods and how it's gonna surprise the hell outta some bear. But, about this time, they saw I was listening and they went to talking Basque. I don't savvy but a few words of their lingo so that was pretty much all she wrote on that score."

"You ever ask Joe about this?"

Phil smiled and shook his head slightly. "I did, but I think he must have had the dumber 'n rocks talk with Stroud."

"What do you think?"

"Oh, I don't think Garmendia would have any problem with rigging up a set gun out in the woods, but you'll play hell getting him to 'fess up to that."

"I figured as much. But just so you know, I'm hopin' to leave you outta this."

Phil's eyes suddenly shifted to his rearview mirror. "I think it's a little too late for that."

I looked up the road. A fast-moving spot of blue was coming towards us. I instantly recognized it. I said, "I'm sorry."

Phil reached for the toothpick that had been bobbing between his lips at the corner of his mouth and threw it on the ground. "Well, I guess we're about to see how this plays out with his highness."

Moments later Stroud's blue pickup came to a stop behind Phil's. He'd barely turned the motor off and he was out of the cab walking quickly towards the space between Phil and I's vehicles. The look in his eyes was intense and hateful. I skipped any social greeting and cut right to it. "I was just coming to see you. Your man died last night."

If Stroud felt bad about hearing this his face didn't show it. He said, "Well then, it seems to me you should be knockin' on this Bolander fella's door, not mine."

Anger took hold of my tongue. "If it wasn't for you, I wouldn't need to be knockin' on anybody's door."

"How's that?"

"Don't play dumb with me. My patience is wearing thin. We both know it was your set gun that killed Teddy Bolander. The only question is, did you personally put the gun out or did you have one of your men do it?"

"Like I've already told you, I didn't have anything to do with this set gun that you're harping about."

In a heated argument, momentum can sometimes have unintended consequences. I came back quick, maybe too quick, I said, "Well. we'll see what Joe Garmendia has to say. I'm thinkin' he might tell a different story."

Stroud flashed a hateful look at Phil and shook his head. He said, "You been tellin' your son-in-law a bunch of lies?"

Phil snorted and tossed his head back slightly. "I ain't told him nuthin' I don't know, but I think he's on to something wantin' to talk to Joe."

Stroud shot back, "Why you loose-lipped sonovabitch."

For a few seconds, Phil looked hard at Stroud. A derisive smile came to his face and then he said, "I'm gonna give you a pass just this one time, but I'm tellin' ya, if you call me anymore names except Mr. Lujack, I'm gonna stomp a mud hole in your ass. Are we clear on that?'

At first, Stroud appeared unable to speak, but then he began being careful how he spoke, "I won't tolerate that, not from no hired hand I won't. You're done. I want you out of my house by noon tomorrow. I'll be by to see that you are and give you a check for what I owe you."

A pall fell over the three of us as the gravity of what Stroud had just done sunk in. Phil and his family had been living where they were for almost 40 years. It is where I had gone to pick up Ellen for our first date. To our kids it was grandpa and grandma's house. There were lots of memories there. I glanced over at Phil. His look said he wasn't about to grovel. I, on the other hand, was drowning in my guilt. I said, "Mr. Stroud, Phil didn't tell me anything that I didn't already know. I learned about the gun you gave Joe to use on the bears in Cedarville."

Stroud scoffed, "I don't know what you're talking about."

I sighed and shook my head. "It'd be quite a story for them to make up."

"Well, there isn't any truth to it."

"I wished you'd reconsider about firing Phil."

Stroud came back quick. "No, I need a man I can trust."

"In matters that are lawful, I think you know that you can."

"No, we're done here. Now, if one of you will move out of the way I've apparently got to go to town and make funeral arrangements for my man."

At the risk of re-igniting Stroud's anger, I said, "Just so you know, an autopsy will have to be completed before the body can be released for burial."

"An autopsy? What the hell for? You know how he died."

Since Stroud wanted to persist in stonewalling me, I came back at him, "Well, I believe he was beat to death and not dragged by his horse as you once claimed. But I want to be sure there was no other underlying reason that might have caused a healthy man like Felipe to die."

"Why, so you can go light on your Bolander friend?"

I looked at Stroud. My voice was curt, "It's protocol. The man died an unnatural death. An official determination has to be made."

Stroud frowned at me and then started walking off. He'd taken only a few steps when he abruptly stopped and turned toward me. He said in a smug tone, "I don't want to see you on my property. You've got no right to be there."

"But I do. Two people are dead and you or Joe Garmendia are directly or indirectly responsible. I'd call that probable cause."

For a moment, Stroud directed a hateful and contempt filled stare at me before slurring the words, "Screw you."

He then got in his pickup and not waiting for either me or Phil to move our vehicles, he bounced into the borrow ditch and out into the sagebrush on the far side of Phil's truck. When he came back into the ditch in front of Phil his rear wheels were spinning furiously, shooting dirt and rock and bits of grass into the air until he reached the pavement and his knobby tires screeched leaving black marks for five or six feet. In spite of not having a home anymore, Phil laughed. "I think ya pissed him off."

"I'm sorry, Phil. I really feel bad about what just happened."

Phil shrugged, "The guy's an asshole. If it didn't happen today it probably would've on down the road."

"But I'm the cause of this."

Phil took a pack of Lucky Strikes from his shirt pocket and shook one out far enough to grasp it with his lips. He said, the cigarette bobbing up and down slightly, "Don't worry about it, I ain't." And then he flipped the lid on his lighter with the Marine Corps emblem on its side and brought life to his cigarette. He went on, blowing a cloud of blue smoke out his window, "When Stroud first came to the valley and bought out Peterson and the others, I could see how he was then. I told Niko that maybe it was time for us to fold our tent and move on to some place else, but neither one of us knew where that place might be so we ended up staying."

"Do you regret it?"

He took a slow, deliberate drag from his cigarette like he was thinking and then exhaled the smoke into his steering wheel. He said, "No, the Gros Ventre has been our home for a long time. It's been good to us but now it's different. Today just kind of woke me up to that fact."

"How do you think Niko will take this?"

Phil removed the cigarette from his mouth and flicked the ash out the window. He smiled and said, "Oh shit, startin' out she's gonna have a hissy fit but I think once she gets that out of her system she'll be ok with whatever we end up doing so long as it don't take her away from you and Ellen and the grandkids."

"You guys could come to our place."

Phil smiled. "That'd be pretty cozy."

As unpleasant thoughts sometimes do, they occur at awkward times but this one seemed to fit the moment. I said, "Roy got his draft notice."

"The hell you say."

"Yeah, came in the mail yesterday."

"How's Roy with it?"

"I don't think he's happy about it, but he's taking it in stride."

Phil appeared to be intently looking at something on his black steering wheel, studying it even, and then he said, "Well, I don't know that this Vietnam deal is a good investment of blood and money, but I guess a fella's gotta do what he's gotta do."

For a second I considered telling him of Ellen trying to get Roy to join the Air Force, but I set it aside knowing that Phil had experienced the same pain as she had years ago. Instead, I came back to the problem at hand. I said, "We'll likely have a room available if you guys want to stay with us till you find a permanent place to land."

Phil laughed. "Thanks for the offer but I'm afraid us two old codgers would just be underfoot. But I appreciate you offering."

"No, seriously you should think about it."

"I did, but you know while we been sittin' here, I had a brain fart."

"How so?"

"Well, I was talkin' to old Jack Barnes the other day and he propositioned me to come run his place on a shares deal. I told him no cause I ain't too much younger than him but, now that I'm homeless, his offer looks a whole lot better."

I wasn't certain what the exact nature of Phil's job with Stroud was but I suspected it was more telling others what to do as opposed to being just a worker bee. I said, "Running Barnes' place could make for a lot of long days."

Phil looked at me pretending to be insulted, "What, you saying I ain't man enough to handle it?"

I laughed. "No, I'm just saying maybe you might want to ratchet down a notch or two, take life a little easier."

Phil came back. "My thinkin' is, if you go to a rocking chair it won't be long till they're shoveling dirt on you."

I shook my head. "Ok, Phil, have it your way but I'll be back this evening and help you move."

"Did you forget? Stroud said you ain't welcome on his property."

I frowned. "I guess he's got me there, but he didn't say anything about Ellen and the kids helping."

Phil grinned. "No, he didn't." He then took a final drag from his cigarette before crushing it in his ashtray. He went on, "I guess the both of us need to get on with our day."

"Yeah, I suppose so."

"I doubt at this time of day that you'll find Garmendia at his house."

"What's your best guess where he'd be?"

"Well, he ain't got anybody to herd those sheep up Badger Creek."

I nodded, "Makes sense. What kind of rig does he drive?"

"Brown '56 Jimmy. It's got a good-sized dent in the left rear fender."

"All right, I'll be on the lookout for it."

Phil started his pickup. He said in a loud voice, "You might wanna be careful with this guy. He's been known to have a temper."

I said, "Thanks for the heads up." And then I said, "Tell Niko I'm sorry for the trouble I'm causing you."

Phil looked at me in kind of a serious way. He said, "You take good care of our daughter and grandkids and we'll call it square."

CHAPTER FIVE

A white metal sign with bold black lettering that read, ROAD NOT MAINTAINED NOV. 1 – MARCH 31 was situated on the side of the road where the pavement ended. There were bullet holes through the center of all the o's belying the fact that the sign had been in place only two years. Its placement was simultaneous with the last ranch along the Gros Ventre and the last stop on the school bus route. Beyond this point there were no fields or houses and not many fences, just wide-open government ground that went on for about 30 miles. A person then encountered more evidence of civilization, although just barely. The need for the sign came about due to an old man and his wife having taken the road during January in the mistaken belief that it would be a shortcut to Great Falls. They might have made it through but someone, maybe somebody related to the sign shooter, switched the signs at the junction with Badger Creek. The old folks made it almost to the mouth of the canyon before they got stuck. To their credit, they had a shovel in their trunk. The man's wife said he'd been working not quite an hour, she guessed, when he just fell face down in the snow and died. The woman spent two nights in the car with her husband froze stiff outside. Fortunately, the third day of her ordeal coincided with the end of the month and a couple of Soil Conservation Service guys in a snow cat coming to measure the snow. When I was finally summoned and rode back in with the snow cat guys to retrieve the man's body, I was taken by how surreal the whole thing seemed. The landscape was a sea of creamy white with the tops of the taller sagebrush peppering the snow. And there in the midst of it was a red '59 Oldsmobile visible only from the door handles up. But today, as I drove by the spot where it had been mired down and the old people had their lives ruined by some senseless prank, it was hot and the road dusty. It caused me to think, to fantasize I guess because there's not a thing a person can do about time gone by, but I thought if only the old people had waited for a day like today. But with Teddy Bolander, hell, if he'd just stumbled going up the hill towards that gun and been just a few seconds later, he'd be alive and Felipe Arriola too and Fred wouldn't be in trouble and the Bolander family wouldn't be in shambles. All because of Joe Garmendia.

It was a few minutes till noon when I turned onto the Porphyry Creek two-track. I was uncertain what I would do if Garmendia denied everything, which is what I expected him to do. At a minimum, I needed to let him know that whoever put out the gun that killed Teddy was in trouble and that sooner or later they would have to pay for their deed. Basically, I needed to appeal to his common sense and conscience, if he had one.

I was getting close to the clearing where Bolanders had their posts piled and had not seen any sign of the sheep. I was beginning to wonder if Garmendia had the nerve to move his sheep camp there when I rolled past a big clump of willows and there it was off to my left about a hundred yards from the road. The camp resembled a pioneer's covered wagon except the ends were enclosed. The front of the wagon had a split wooden door so that the bottom half could stay closed while the top remained open or closed. The back end was solid wood except for a small rectangular window that, when slid open, allowed a breeze to flow through.

Heavy white canvas that conformed to wooden ribs arching overhead enclosed the wagon box. It appeared Garmendia, or somebody, was home as light blue smoke was drifting up from the rusty tin stovepipe that protruded above the roof of the sheep camp. The brown Jimmy that Phil had told me about was parked nearby. I turned off the two-track in the direction of the camp and began idling across the green stubble that was pock marked with ground squirrel holes and a carpet of sheep manure. Two black and white dogs stood up in the shade of the wagon and then came running towards me barking excitedly. Both halves of the camp's door were open. Moments later, a stocky muscular looking man with short coal black hair and bushy eyebrows stepped outside. As I got closer, I sized him up. He was a head shorter but probably weighed as much as I did. These days that was about 215. Most importantly, though, was he appeared to be 10 to 15 years younger than me. I stopped about 20 feet short of the camp and got out of my truck. One of the dogs came up to me and began sniffing at my pant leg while the other pissed on my left rear tire. I said, while looking the man straight in the eye, "Afternoon, I'm Sheriff Yarnell from over at Fremont. You wouldn't happen to be Joe Garmendia, would ya?"

The man snorted in kind of a sarcastic way. He said, keeping the same cocky attitude, "Why are you looking for this guy?"

I said, "You know, if you are Mr. Garmendia, it isn't going to help your cause any by playing this little cat and mouse game."

Garmendia came back in a smug tone. "My boss said you'd be coming."

"Then you know why I'm here?"

"I know why you think that you should be here, but I didn't have anything to do with that kid getting shot. If you're looking for somebody to arrest why don't you go get that crazy guy that attacked my cousin. Mr. Stroud says he's pretty bad off."

It instantly occurred to me that telling this guy his cousin had died would be like pouring gas on a smoldering fire. I nodded, "Yeah, I was sorry to hear that."

Garmendia smirked, "I'll bet."

I frowned. Being civil, at least with me, was not part of who this guy was. I said, "Well Joe, I guess we might as well just get down to business. I've been told that you've been killing bears with a set gun."

The anger within him suddenly became more visible. I could see it in his black eyes as he glared at me. Even the muscles in his face had tensed up beneath the dark stubble of his whiskers. I'd struck a nerve but his response was slow in coming. After a few seconds, he defended himself, "That's bullshit. Who told you that?"

"I can't say at this point."

"I got a right to know cuz it's a damned lie."

"If we go to trial, you'll find out."

Joe shouted back at me, "Trial. You're full of shit if you think that you're going to arrest me." And then he paused and drew off some tobacco juice from the lump in his left cheek and spit it defiantly on the ground between us. "I ain't goin' nowhere with you."

It was like he'd drawn a line in the dirt and was daring me to cross it. Right now I would be hard-pressed to legally do that. Even though everything that I'd learned thus far pointed to Joe as the person ultimately responsible for Teddy's death, I had my doubts that I could get a warrant for his arrest without the actual gun that was used. And then, like it was another incriminating arrow pointing at him, I saw from the corner of my left eye a mostly yellow box of cartridges on the dash of the Jimmy. It was a good-sized box, bigger than for a 30-30. The end of it was pointed such that it was questionable if I could read the caliber, which I couldn't, but Joe didn't know that. I said, nodding towards the box, "Do you own a 45-70?"

A flash of panic came and went in Joe's face as he followed my eyes to his pickup. He said, "what's that got to do with anything?"

"A 45-70 is what I heard you've been using on the bears." And then I added just to work on his conscience, "Judging from the size of the hole in that kid's chest it had to have been made by a large caliber gun, like a 45-70."

Joe was un-phased. "That might be but it wasn't my gun."

"So, you do own a 45-70?"

Unconsciously, I suppose, his eyes darted to a horse that was tied to an aspen tree a little way beyond the sheep camp. The horse was saddled. On the side facing us, I could see a rifle in a scabbard. I said, looking towards the horse, "That your rifle over there?"

Joe nervously spit again. Some of the spittle fell to his chin. He wiped it off with the back of his hand and then brushed that away on the leg of his dark blue Levis. He said, with renewed anger in his voice, "Now who's playing cat and mouse? I know what you're doing."

"What's that?"

He looked at me like I was purposely being stupid and said, "I think you figure if you keep badgerin' me about this whole deal that I'll just up and tell you I did something that I didn't."

As I looked at the horse, I recalled the soft bark of the aspen and the slice marks from where the set gun had been wired. From there, my mind's eye went on visualizing what that wire likely did to the finish of the rifle's stock. I said, as I started walking towards the horse, "Joe, we can clear this up right now. I'll just take a quick look at your gun and that might settle this matter."

He stepped in front of me. "You ain't got any right to look at my gun."

I said, "I got probable cause that it was used in a crime. Now you need to move aside." Joe snorted in disgust and took a step back but no sooner had I started by him when I felt his hand on my right shoulder. I looked at him quick and hard. "You don't want to be touching me. That'd be interfering with the law."

He scowled sarcastically, "Says you?"

I could see it in his eyes there was a fight coming. He was just working up the courage, little by little, until he could justify discarding what remained of his common sense that hadn't been destroyed by his fear of going to jail. I said calmly, but in a tone that he knew I meant business, "Move away from me, Joe. In fact, why don't you go stand by your pickup where I can see you."

He looked at me for a few seconds like he wasn't going anywhere before finally starting towards his pickup. When he was a few feet from it and about ten feet from me I continued on to the horse. I was about half-way there when I heard footsteps coming fast behind me. I was barely turned around when Joe drove his right shoulder into my chest knocking me off my feet. He immediately capitalized on his advantage and landed a hard, right hand squarely in the middle of my face. I literally felt my nose break to the side. Seconds later I could taste the saltiness of my blood as it filtered through my moustache onto my lips and down the back of my throat. Three more successive blows stunned me to the point I couldn't retaliate before he was sitting on my chest and choking me. His hands were big and meaty. They felt like a snare that kept getting tighter and tighter. His eyes were wild like nothing I'd ever seen. Droplets of spit, laden with tobacco juice, sprayed from his mouth onto my face as he ranted above me, "You sonovabitch, I'll teach you to stick your nose where it don't belong." The pain in my throat was intense. I could hardly breath. I was afraid that I was about to die when the fear of it released a wave of adrenaline in my body. In that instant I was able to free my right arm from beneath Joe's knee. With everything I had, I brought my fist up and hit him in the face. The blow caused him to loosen his grip momentarily, to the point I could land a second and third punch and then roll to my side causing him to tumble off of me. Although I was gasping for air, I felt like I would at least survive when, suddenly, Joe pulled a hunting knife from a sheath on his right hip. He raised the knife and lunged toward me while still on his knees. Laying on my back I kicked at him while I fumbled to undo the snap strap over my pistol. I felt the knife go into my calf but it was a dull sensation, distant and vague to the possibility I might die. And then, I honestly don't remember pulling the trigger nor really even the sound. What stands out most was the surprised look on Joe's face as he folded up like a rag doll and collapsed on top of me. His head landed on my chest just short of my chin. In spite of the horror of his wide-open eyes staring at me, I felt pinned and unable to move. And then he gave an involuntary last gasp, a gurgling escape of the remaining air in his lungs. Instantly, the strength to catapult his body to the side came to me. I sat up and scooted back a few feet, not so much because he might still be alive but mostly to distance myself from what I had done. I sat there, still clutching my .38, staring intently at Joe. A blood stain that wasn't real big, maybe three or four inches across, occupied an area on his brown tee shirt right about where his heart would be. In the center of it was a neat round hole. My heart was hammering hard enough to be winning the pain contest between my broken nose, loose teeth and the stab wound in my right calf. I felt sick to my stomach and unsteady, trembly I guess. In 24 years of being in law enforcement I'd never had to fire my gun, let alone kill someone. To have to do it now and add what I was seeing to the parade of unpleasantness that too often came through my mind in the middle of the night made me mad at Joe. The herder's dogs came over, curious as to what had happened. They stopped short of the body and then stretched their necks so as to bring their noses within an inch or two of it. Within seconds they seemed satisfied with what they'd found and went back to the shade beneath the sheep camp. I wondered if Joe hadn't been good to the dogs or that's just how they were, but then I recalled how Teddy's dog had been and a little bit of the guilt I was feeling for having killed Joe melted away. Beyond me, Joe's horse nickered. I glanced up at it and in that instant saw the rifle in its scabbard and heard the naysayer in my mind shout out, *You better hope that gun is a 45-70 and its got wire markings on it or you're gonna be in deep shit.* I rolled to my hands and knees and started to get up. It was only then that I felt the effects of having my calf muscle impaled on the blade of Joe's knife. The pain was deep and seemed to consume my right leg from the knee to my ankle. Still, the fear that I wouldn't find a 45-70, or worse yet no wire marks on it, caused me to hobble to the horse. Reaching it, I rested my right hand on the seat of the saddle and shifted most of my weight to my left leg as I pulled the rifle from the scabbard. Within seconds I saw the 45-70 stamped on the barrel, but then my eyes immediately settled on that part of the stock just back from the lever. It was slightly marred but there was no evidence of baling wire having dug into the wood. I shook my head as I muttered aloud, "Oh, shit." Panic consumed me for several seconds until I turned the rifle over to look at the other side of the stock. There, as plain as day, were the worry marks of the wire. Some relief came quickly to me as if God had taken his foot off the accelerator that fed my fear. It occurred to me the gun would be marked this way because there would have been more tension on the side of the stock facing away from the tree trunk. Regardless, with these marks, the box of shells on the dash of the Jimmy and George Morgan's testimony, I had my probable cause for wanting to examine Joe's rifle.

I took the gun and limped back to where Joe's body was lying. A raven, in its uncanny way of knowing there might be a free meal in the offing, had perched itself in a big ponderosa pine on the other side of Joe's pickup. He was cackling, I suppose, to let others of his kind know that lunch was about to commence. The possibility of him descending upon Joe and pecking away at his eyes and exposed fleshy parts was real, as I knew that I would likely have to drive all the way down to the mouth of Badger Creek to get radio reception. And there would be ants, and beetles too that would enjoy the feast before I returned. I had little choice but to go into Joe's sheep camp in search of a blanket or something to wrap him in.

After putting the rifle in the cab of my truck, I went to the sheep camp and stepped up inside. I was immediately confronted with the odor of burnt meat and coffee. To my right, on a small wood burning stove, was a cast iron frying pan with three slices of Spam and a diced potato in it. Joe had been in the process of cooking his lunch, which was now charcoal like. A silver colored metal coffee pot with a glass knob in its lid sat next to the pan over the hot part of the stove. The dark frothy liquid pulsed up into the knob and the pour spout. It was close to boiling over. I moved the pot and pan to the right side of the stove where it was cooler. The meat ceased to sizzle, and the coffee's pulse slowed like a dying man. An eerie feeling came over me as I stood there and looked around. A Big Ben alarm clock sat on a small slab of a table that folded down from the side of the wagon. Its bare wood was dark and worn smooth by years of use. A single wooden leg supported it. The clock's ticking was loud and seemed mournful to me. Close to it, clustered together, was a bottle of ketchup and cardboard salt and pepper shakers that were meant to be thrown away when they were empty, a little orange packet of tobacco papers and a red can of Prince Albert tobacco. A blue plate with red flowers around its edge, a knife and fork, two biscuits just lying there, a half full cup of coffee and a white saucer with a partial stick of butter on it were all there too. A dead man's lunch. The naysayer in my mind shouted out to me, *if you'd not turned your back on him he wouldn't have gotten the drop on you. He'd be alive, maybe not eating his lunch but you wouldn't feel like you do now.* I sighed and looked away from the table, as I did several drops of blood broke free from my lips and fell to the floor. They added to the splattering that I'd already created there. The blood coming from my nose had eased off from a steady flow to oozing. The front of my shirt was more blood stain than not. On the shelf to the left of the stove was a roll of toilet paper. I unrolled some of it and formed a couple of plugs for my nostrils and inserted them. It stopped the bleeding but there was no breathing through my nose. Across the back of the room was Joe's bed. The July issue of Playboy was lying on it. On the shelf above his bed was a stack of what appeared to be more skin magazines and a good number of paperbacks. A kerosene chimney lantern sat on a shelf near the head of the bed. It struck me how lonely herding sheep was. Through the open window I could hear the aspen leaves gently rustle and then die away. And out the front door the raven cawed impatiently. Some pitchy wood in the stove popped and all the while the clock on the table never missed a beat in reminding a person of just how alone he was. Collectively, it was the kind of solitude that, in large doses, required a special person. Years ago, as a young deputy living in the county's cabin in Cedarville, I'd gotten my share of loneliness, but I had the Antler Bar to go to when it got bad. But here, if a man steps outside his sheep wagon, he's just going to get another helping.

There were no sheets on Joe's bed, just two blankets. A light one against the mattress and a heavier dark green one to sleep under. I grabbed a fistful of the top cover and pulled it off the bed, wadding it up in my arms. I hadn't quite made it to the door when I heard the rumble of an engine coming up the road. I whispered aloud, "If that's Stroud he's gonna go haywire." I stepped outside and waited for the mystery noise to show itself. Moments later, Myron Cheevers' pickup emerged from the trees and then came to an abrupt stop as he spotted my vehicle and then started across the clearing towards me. I was holding the blanket in front of me so the blood on my shirt was not visible but when he was about 100 feet away, I could see the look on his face evolve from curiosity to shock. He stopped next to me. Out his window he shouted, "Holy shit, Hoss. You look like you been in a train wreck."

I nodded. "It's pretty bad, Myron."

Just then he caught sight of Joe's body and a raven that was on the ground hopping towards it. He said, dead serious now, "What happened?"

"Stroud's man jumped me. As you can see, I didn't fare too well and then things escalated into a knife fight and I ended up shooting him."

"Him?"

"Joe Garmendia. He's Stroud's sheep foreman. I was told by one of the locals that he's the guy who put out the set gun."

Myron appeared a little irritated. He hesitated and then said, "I thought you were going to share with me whatever you learned about this deal?"

"I learned this just out of the blue at the Lumberjack this morning."

I could see that Myron was not entirely satisfied with my response but he moved on, getting out of his pickup. He said, "Ya got any help comin'?"

"Not yet, I wanted to cover this guy before I go find a spot that I can get out on the radio."

Myron stepped close and took hold of the blanket. "Why don't you let me do that and you go call for help."

I held onto the blanket just long enough so as to not appear eager to take Myron up on his offer and then I let go of it. Before I could tell him thanks, his eyes got big as he saw the front of my shirt. He said in a concerned tone, "Are you sure you're all right to drive?"

I nodded. "It looks worse than it is."

Myron grinned, "Well, Hoss, lookin' any worse than you do is usually called dead."

I returned his grin. "I appreciate your help, Myron. I'll be back as soon as I can." I then started limping towards my pickup. Myron apparently took note of my limp and likely the bloodstain on the back of my pants leg. He shouted after me, "Dammit, Andy, why don't you just sit yourself down. I'll go call for help. You can ride out of here in the ambulance."

I shouted over my shoulder. "I'll be alright. Besides, that fella over there has already got dubs on the ambulance ride." Myron went silent, apparently thinking it was a lost cause to get me to stay and him go. It was a bit of an effort getting in my pickup which I had anticipated, but what I hadn't expected was how painful it would be to work the gas pedal. But then I'd never had a knife blade stuck into my calf to the point it stopped only because it hit my shin bone. Needless to say, the ride out to the mouth of the canyon had me second guessing my decision to turn down Myron's offer.

At the junction of the Badger Creek road and CR29 I pulled over. The reception here wasn't the best but I had gotten out in the past. I was about to reach for my mic when Millie came over the speaker. "604 this is Gros Ventre base."

I keyed the mic. "Go ahead, Millie."

"Hi Andy, the district attorney called this morning. He want's you to call him just as soon as you get to a phone."

I sighed and shook my head. "Did he say what he wanted?"

"No, he just said he needed to talk to you today."

"Alright, Millie but it's gonna have to wait till later. I've run into some trouble out here."

"Are you alright?"

"Not entirely. I'm near where the Bolanders were cuttin' posts. I need for Tyler to head this way and probably somebody from the highway patrol and I guess it'd be good if Raymond O'Leary came too, but tell him to come in the county's ambulance, it has higher clearance."

"You're scaring me, Andy."

"Sorry, don't mean to."

"Is somebody dead?"

"Yes."

"Was it an accident?"

"No, I shot him on purpose."

I knew Millie wanted to probe me for the details, but she knew better than to ask that over the radio. She said, "All right, Andy, I'll get these folks headed your way. Anything else?"

I thought for a brief moment how it would look with my deputy, the county coroner and the highway patrol all going through Cedarville and on up the valley. It would make for juicy gossip and even though there were no phones in the outlying valley, there were in Cedarville and the ranger station at the edge of town. I had little doubt that half-baked speculation would get back to Fremont and possibly the forest service office where Ellen worked, before I got home. I said, "If you would, Millie, call Ellen. Tell her I had some trouble out here but that I'm ok and I'll be a little late getting' home."

"Sure, Andy, I'll call her just as soon as I get these other folks going."

After clearing myself, it felt good to just sit there in the quiet and drain off some of the tension. I tried to soak up the peacefulness of a meadowlark singing from its sagebrush perch nearby and the steady raspy clatter of grasshoppers as they flew from place to place in the hot sun. I suspected why the DA wanted to talk to me, but I wondered if when he learned of what had happened today that might change. In the silence I began to question my actions and wished that Myron had been there with me. Things would be different now. I wouldn't be sitting here in pain, with sweat running down my face, replaying in my mind the fight with Joe and regretting, like nothing before in my life, that I had killed him. It was a feeling, a fantasy I guess, that if I took on enough guilt it would square things with God, my conscience, and anybody else that mattered. So far, that didn't seem to be working. No, I couldn't be alone with my thoughts right now. I reached over and turned the volume up on my AM radio. A commercial for Bob's Big Sky Steakhouse in Great Falls was playing. It took me to the time year before last that Ellen and I drove up there for our anniversary. We had dinner at Bob's and spent the night at the Holiday Inn and had breakfast the next morning at a Sambo's. Take away the silence and like dominos falling, my mind was filled with other things. I turned my truck around and started back up the Badger creek road pretending to be interested in the weather for tomorrow; clear and sunny with a high of 84 in Great Falls.

CHAPTER SIX

Porphyry creek runs down the bottom of a canyon with steep timber covered mountains to either side of it. Because of this, it was not quite six o'clock and shadows were beginning to form on the side of the canyon where Joe's camp was located. I had gone over frontwards and backwards with the highway patrol and Raymond O'Leary how it was that I came to kill Joe. They both seemed satisfied with what I had to say and gave the impression that Joe deserved what he got. But then, when we were wrapping up, it was Raymond, of all people, who said, *it's too bad you were alone. I don't think this guy would've tried to take on two people.* This caused Myron to give me an awkward glance and me to not look at either him or Raymond, as I wanted to tell the both of them to *go screw themselves* since we'd already been over how it was that I came to be here by myself. It also occurred to me that this was no innocent observation on Raymond's part and that he was getting back at me for calling him on his indiscretion at the Conoco. But then none of this mattered as the muffled rumble of a pickup methodically working its way up the two-track road across the meadow became audible. All eyes turned towards the noise wondering who was about to come out of the trees.

Myron was first to speak, "Well, now the shit's gonna hit the fan."

Unaware of who was coming, the highway patrolman said, "Why's that?"

I said, "This is Joe Garmendia's boss." And then I spontaneously hissed, "You've got to be kidding me."

Myron looked at me and snorted, "Hoss, this ain't lookin' good for the home team."

I shook my head, forgetting how it might be perceived by the occupants of Stroud's pickup. I said, "Stroud showing up here doesn't surprise me, but Ed Peck?"

Myron said sarcastically, "Well, it is an election year."

Stroud stopped his pickup just short of the ambulance. He was quick to get out as was the district attorney. He looked at our group and singled me out before shouting, "You got Joe in there?"

I looked at Stroud and nodded. "He tried to kill me. I had no choice but to fight back."

Stroud scoffed. "You had a choice in coming here didn't ya? You had no business being here,"

"But I did, Mr. Stroud. You know I did."

Stroud scoffed. "What I know is Fred Bolander confessed to you that he beat my herder to death and you won't arrest him. That's what I know."

Ed Peck chimed in, "Is that right, Andy?"

I nodded. "Yeah, Fred told me at the funeral home that he got into it with the herder. It was just after we'd unloaded his dead son. I didn't figure it was the time or the place to arrest him."

Stroud jumped in, "Well, my herder died last night which makes Bolander a murderer but what do you do today? Instead of arresting him you come out snooping around my camp and goad one of my men into a fight so you can kill him."

Rage instantly consumed me. "You idiot, Stroud. I –"

Peck attempted to interrupt, "Andy, you need to calm down."

I shot back at the DA, "Calm down my ass. Look at me. I came damned close to being the one riding back to town in a body bag."

Being a short somewhat rotund person, Peck was easily intimidated by other men but, in this instance, he had the authority of his position on his side. He adjusted his black plastic frame glasses and looked at me with a peculiar arrogance seemingly ignorant of the fact I now had rolls of gauze plugging both my nostrils, my eyes were black, my lower lip was split and the front of my shirt was soaked with blood. He said, "You don't want to forget who you're talking to."

Over the years, I'd always been able to pretty much control my emotions regardless of the situation but, on this occasion, I don't know what happened. I shouted, "Why you dumbass, what part of a near death experience do you not understand?"

Peck was taken aback but not to the degree I thought he would be. Instead, he struck a casual pose by putting his hands in the pockets of his dress slacks and resting the brown oxford on his right foot on a small rock in front of him. He said, "Andy, I know you're upset but, unless you want to elevate this to a higher level, you'd be well advised to settle down."

Before I could answer, Stroud jumped in, "Well, I'll just say this, if the Sheriff here continues to stonewall on arresting this Bolander guy, I'll be making a call over to Helena. We'll see what the Attorney General has to say about all this."

A fearful look immediately came over Peck's face. "Now Orville, I told you on the way out here that we'd handle this. There's no need for you to call Helena."

"Then, by hell, Bolander better be going to jail in the morning. He's wandering around scot-free and two of my men are dead because of him."

Myron cut in. "Well, while you're pointin' fingers you'd better not be standing in front of any mirrors."

Stroud gave Myron a look like he was a hillbilly fool. "So, what's that supposed to mean?"

"It was your damned set gun that started this whole mess."

"I had nothing to do with any set gun."

Myron scoffed, "Yeah, and I'm the Queen of England."

Recalling what George Morgan had told me, I said, "So, Joe just took it upon himself to put your gun out there?"

"Who says it was my gun?"

Even though I suspected George would be reluctant to get involved, I said it anyway, "I know a fella that'll likely testify the gun I took off that saddle horse over there is the same one you bought at auction."

Stroud was silent, his eyes glaring back at me. Finally, he said, "I loaned my rifle to Joe in case he caught a coyote or bear in the sheep. I never told him to use it as a set gun."

Myron threw in, "Well, we'll see about that."

Stroud shot a hateful look toward Myron. "Yeah, well mister fish cop, you just do that but you'll play hell giving me a ticket for a set gun. The only person that you'd have even a ghost of a chance in doing that to is dead, courtesy of your pal here."

I said, my voice loud and angry, "He didn't give me a choice."

Ed Peck stepped between us. "Gentlemen, we're getting slightly off subject." He paused, purposely not looking my direction but his body language suggesting that he was collecting himself to address me and then he turned my way. "Andy, I'll have you an arrest warrant for Bolander by ten o'clock in the morning. I expect you to serve it tomorrow."

To his credit, Raymond said, "Teddy's service is day after tomorrow."

Stroud caught Peck's eye. "We're talking murder here."

I scoffed. "This was a fight that just sprung up from too much raw emotion. Fred Bolander is not a killer. Things just got out of hand."

Peck said, "Regardless, Andy, he's got to answer for what he did. A man's dead."

I looked at Peck. I was hoping to see some sign of reluctance in his face but there was none. What I could see though, was he was more fearful of Stroud calling Helena than he was the blowback for arresting Fred before he could bury his son. But in this same instant, it occurred to me that most people in the county wouldn't know what was said here in this little meadow on Porphyry creek. Nor would they know that a couple of years ago, Peck had told me after a few drinks at the Legion bar that he didn't *intend on spending his entire life in this little shithole of a town.* He called me the next day to say that, *you know that was just the liquor talking, don't you?* I lied and allowed him to ease his conscience saying, *Oh, I know Ed, those Coke hi-balls can cause a man's tongue to run away with its self.* But I didn't believe that for a second. My take on Ed was, that having graduated from the UCLA school of law, he saw Gros Ventre county as beneath him even though his grandparents lived in Fremont. They were good people, good enough I guess that Ed got his foot in the door in county politics. Seeing the writing on the wall, I said, "I'll be by your office at ten tomorrow morning."

Stroud smirked as he said to Peck, "Well good, now that's settled I need to get down to the home place and get somebody to replace Joe before it gets dark." He then looked at me as if to shower me with guilt. "I've got a thousand head of sheep here with no herder."

They turned, the two of them, and started back towards Stroud's pickup. The silence that followed was broken only when Peck stepped in some green sheep shit causing him to swear. Raymond allowed them to disappear into the trees before he started out in the ambulance followed by my deputy and the highway patrolman. Their exodus left just Myron and me. He said, "You headed for the hospital or the barn?"

I managed a weak smile. "I suppose I'll swing by the hospital first."

"Are you ok to make it that far?"

"Oh yeah, I'm gonna head out after I tend to Joe's animals."

"The sheep?"

I laughed. "No, his dogs and horse."

Myron was a little embarrassed. He said, "I'll help ya."

"Fine, if you wanna unsaddle and tend to the horse I'll feed the dogs."

In their way the animals showed their appreciation that we'd stayed and looked after them. If there was one bright spot in this day it was this feeling that I'd done at least one good thing. We convoyed on down Badger creek to 29 and turned south toward Cedarville. It was full on dusk when we went by Phil's place. It was a beehive of activity. There were several pickups there that I didn't recognize. Each was towing a big stock trailer that people were busy filling with stuff from the house. They were like soldier ants, these friends that had accrued from 40 years in the valley. I was glad to see that Phil had help in moving, but at the same time, my anger for Stroud boiled up again.

CHAPTER SEVEN

Our little country hospital didn't have an emergency room entrance. If you were in need of immediate medical care you just walked in the front door like everybody else. Unfortunately, my arrival coincided with the tail end of visiting hours. A plump. middle-aged woman with graying auburn hair accompanied by her also plump teenage daughter rounded the corner from the hallway where the patient rooms, all six of them, were located. I was standing at the front counter and since I had no other clothes but the ones I was wearing, I still looked pretty much like I did right after Joe and I had fought. From the corner of my left eye, I recognized the woman but pretended to not see her coming. When she was nearly to me, she said, "I heard you killed a man today."

I turned away from the receptionist and looked at the woman who seemed unphased by my appearance, whereas her daughter became visibly uncomfortable. I felt like I was entitled to respond with something as crude and insensitive as she had just done. It wasn't like I had been deer hunting and had shot a nice buck, but I said, "How is it you come by this information, Mrs. Tutweiller?"

"My husband called me from the Antler Bar a little while ago. He said Orville Stroud came in there tonight hopping mad. Said you'd just killed Joe Garmendia. And then my husband said Stroud went into this tirade how Fred Bolander had killed another one of his herders and your father in-law was conspiring against him, so he had to fire him and now here he was having to haul one of his men out of the bar after he'd just gave him a few days off." She paused and smiled, not sympathetically, and added, "My husband said that old stew-bum was drunker than a million dollars. He said Stroud took him to the café part of the Antler and tried to get the guy to eat something but that just made him sick. I guess the fella didn't make it to the bathroom in time. My husband said the cook was using language that he didn't think most women even knew. He said it got to be a circus in there and not a fun one. Said it made him want to come home."

At about this point, it dawned on me that Ruth Tutweiller didn't give a hoot about Joe Garmendia being dead or the obvious fact that I was injured. Him and I were just gossip to her. She would not be seeing Joe's face in her dreams tonight. I, on the other hand, probably wouldn't even sleep. I said to her, fully aware that I hadn't responded to her probe about my killing Joe, "If you'll excuse me, Mrs. Tutweiller, I've got to get checked in." Peripherally, I could see that she frowned at me before walking away.

They cleaned my stab wound before closing it with 11 stitches and giving me a shot of antibiotic and another for tetanus. To quote the doctor, who'd grown up on a ranch north of Fremont before going off and getting educated, *God only knows how many bloated sheep this fella skinned with that knife he stuck you with.*

It was straight up ten o'clock when I left the hospital parking lot. I had prescriptions for an antibiotic and a painkiller but there was no place open to fill them. I'd told the night dispatcher to call Ellen and tell her not to bother coming up to the hospital, that my injuries didn't amount to much and I would be home soon. My motives, however, were not totally unselfish. With everything that had gone on

I had not been able to tell her about my chance meeting with her father and Stroud that had resulted in her father getting fired. Even though her mother worked part-time at the store in Cedarville, I knew that she would be too proud to call her daughter and ask for help in moving given the drive out to the Gros Ventre and the fact that I was forbidden to set foot on Stroud's land. I knew when I got home I'd be chastised, but hopefully in a good way.

As I expected, the lights were on in the kitchen when I parked next to Roy's car. I'd barely gotten out of my pickup when the three of them came out of the house. Ellen had her arms out to hug me but suddenly stopped short as the light from the kitchen window hit my chest. She gasped, and said, almost a whimper, "This is nothing serious?"

Although a nurse had cleaned my face, there was nothing she could do for my shirt which most likely would be permanently stained. I said, "I didn't want to totally ruin your night by having you come to the hospital."

Ellen's demeanor became almost defiant. She looked up at me. "Oh right, Andy, like we're just going to sit here watching tv knowing that you've had to kill a man today and oh, by the way, you're going to swing by the hospital on your way home. You big oaf, we'd rather be where you're at than sit here wondering."

Emma, who was the spitting image of her mother with dark eyes and long black hair, chimed in. "Yeah, dad." Roy, on the other hand, seemed to be taking my side and remained quiet.

In spite of the blood Ellen hugged me, pressing the side of her face to my chest. My chin rested on the top of her head. I whispered, "I'm sorry."

Ellen pushed back slightly and looked up at me for a kiss. It was only then that she noticed my swollen nose, split lip and the blackness beneath my left eye. She grimaced. "Not hurt, huh? What else are you not telling me?"

I said, "We'll talk," and then I leaned down and kissed her.

We filed into the near darkness of the garage with me doing my best not to limp. Along the way, Emma said, "Are you hungry? I brought home burgers and fries from work."

I really didn't feel like eating, especially with my lip and a couple of teeth still seeping blood. But there was more to it than that. In my mind's eye was a litany of all the unpleasant images that had led up to Joe lying on a metal table over at O'Leary's funeral home. It was like I had a viewfinder pushed against my eyes with someone else in charge of it and they kept pulling the lever on the side over and over and over. It just didn't lend itself to my wanting to eat, a beer sounded better. My hesitation caused Emma to add, "Actually, dad, it's a cheeseburger. I know how you like cheeseburgers."

The father side of me came back, "That sounds great, sweetie. I appreciate your doing that."

From behind me, Emma said, "I'll probably need to put it into the toaster oven for a minute or so to warm it up."

As we stepped inside where the light was good and I would be on display, I said, "I'll be back in a minute. I'm gonna change my clothes."

Ellen, who was walking next to me said, "I bet you want a beer with that burger?"

I forced a weak smile. "Well, aren't you the mind reader."

Ellen smiled and squeezed my side. "It'll be ready when you come back."

I briefly pulled her into my side and then let her go as I walked on. Roy, who'd stepped around his mother and I, got his first look at my face in the light. I caught his eye as he looked me over. I wanted to believe that what I saw in his face wasn't shame or embarrassment but I couldn't convince myself otherwise. Every son wants to think his old man is the toughest guy around. Joe Garmendia had destroyed that fantasy today. And then he saw the blood on my pants. "What happened to your leg?"

My intent hadn't been to play the martyr by not being totally forthright about all that had happened to me, but rather I didn't want to worry my family. It wasn't so much these injuries as it was the possibility that one day I wouldn't come home, that it'd be me lying on the metal table at O'Leary's. Over the years, every time the news reported a law officer being killed Ellen would suggest that I get into a different line of work. This conversation would repeat itself for several days with me responding, *it's all I've ever known.* I said to Roy, "The guy stabbed me."

Roy glanced down at my calf. "He stabbed you?"

I could see the perplexed look in his eyes. I said, "He jumped me from behind. We ended up on the ground and –" I hesitated, not wanting to put into words the image of me lying on the ground like a turtle on its back kicking at Joe. It just seemed to reinforce the idea that I hadn't equated myself very well in the fight. I concluded, "and he stabbed me."

Roy's expression indicated he was still trying to visualize how that could take place when Ellen said, "Honey, it's almost ten-thirty, you better go change."

The realization that I didn't want to talk about the fight was full upon me. It would be difficult, I knew, to come back in a few minutes and pick up where Roy and I had left off. So, I said mostly to Emma, "You know, I think I'm going to take a shower. There's no need for you to wait on me with warming that cheeseburger, I can do that when I'm ready."

Emma, who is always so eager to please me, seemed a little hurt but it couldn't be helped. She said simply, "Ok, dad."

As much as I didn't want to create the impression that I didn't want to talk to my family or eat Emma's cheeseburger I retraced my steps to the fridge and got a cold Budweiser. Anticipating my need, Emma dug the bottle opener out of the silverware drawer and handed it to me. I took it, opened my beer and handed it back. I said, "Seriously you guys don't need to wait up for me."

Ellen sensed what I was feeling, I supposed, as she said, "It's time for Johnny Carson. We'll be in the living room. Feel free to join us if you want."

I nodded, "Ok, we'll see."

The bright lights above the bathroom mirror gave me the first good look at myself since I'd shaved this morning, which now seemed like a very long time ago. The injuries made me appear older than my salt and pepper moustache or the gray hair around my temples suggested. It caused me to doubt myself. *I should have been able to get the upper hand on that guy. There shouldn't have been a need for me to shoot him.* I sighed and looked back at myself with contempt. *No, what you should have done is not turn your back on him. What you should have done is heeded Phil's warning and had Myron go with you. That's what you should have done.* I paused and looked even more closely at my reflection wondering, truly wondering, if now that I'd killed a man if I would look different to people. I suspected there'd be whispers and finger pointing and speculation about this *dark side* people always knew that I possessed. In the bars, at the CO-OP, probably even at the Coffee Cup Café where my mother had worked, before she died, this whole affair between Joe and I would be a welcome diversion from the price of barley. They could second guess it and pick it apart as only those totally immune from the emotion of it all could. In my mind's eye I could hear them laugh and say, *Yeah, old Yarnell was getting' his ass handed to him by that sheepherder up until he shot him.* I sighed as I shook my head and turned away from the mirror and began undressing. Today would forever be like a gaudy tattoo acquired during an impetuous moment.

I stood in the shower until the hot water ran cold, something that I'd told the kids they weren't supposed to do. Even though I knew it was a temporary façade, the hot water seemed to draw out the tension and allow me to soap and scrub my moustache several times until the water in my hands came away clean. I changed into a yellow tee shirt with blue lettering that read across the front, Montana State University. All of my clothes lay in a heap on the bathroom floor. I briefly considered putting the bloody stuff in cold water to try and get the stains out but, in the end, I gathered it all up, even my shorts and the one sock with no blood on it and took it to the trash. The bloodstains might have washed out, but I knew that I didn't want to wear these clothes ever again. Even if there was the slightest speck of blood. I just wanted to erase today from my memory.

By the time I came out of the bathroom for good, Roy and Emma had abandoned Johnny Carson in favor of radios in their rooms. As I came into the living room, Ellen got up from the couch. "Are you ready for your cheeseburger?"

I managed a weak grin, "Another beer sounds good but I suppose I should make the effort."

She started towards the kitchen. "Beer on an empty stomach will make you sick."

The image of Ruth Tutweiller telling of Stroud's hired man trying to put food in a stomach full of beer came to mind. I said as I trailed after her and took a seat at the white formica topped table. "I guess a fella needs just the right amounts to make it work."

Ellen put my food on a plate and stuck it in the toaster oven that sat on the kitchen counter to the right of the refrigerator. She said opening the fridge door, "you want some ice tea or a coke or a glass of milk or-"

"I'll take another Bud, please."

Ellen said nothing as she got the beer, opened it and handed it to me. I took a long drink.

She said, "Do you feel any better after your shower?"

"Maybe on the outside I do."

"I guess it's a start."

"Yeah, I suppose it is, but I can tell you, I don't know that I'll ever be shed of today."

Ellen looked over at the timer on the little oven and then for a few seconds we both listened to its whirring sound and in the other room Johnny Carson doing his *The Great Kreskin* bit. Finally, Ellen said, "You did nothing wrong, Andy. This man brought this on himself."

I gave a little sigh and then took another drink of beer. I could feel Ellen's eyes on me and then she added, "It's not your fault. He was trying to kill you. You had no choice."

I snapped at her, "I should never have turned my back on him."

A look of disbelief came over Ellen's face. "You're an officer of the law. People should respect that."

I uttered a short laugh. "I don't think guys like Joe Garmendia have a lot of respect for authority. Your dad even warned me about him."

A sudden look of awareness came to Ellen's eyes. "When did you talk to my dad?"

I was not trying to hide the fact that I'd gotten her father fired, it was more that she had caught me off-guard so reflex took over. I said simply, "This morning on the road north of Cedarville."

"Did he tell you that he's taken a new job? I knew he had another offer but I didn't think he was interested in it. I guess he changed his mind and when he told Stroud, it made him so mad that he wants my folks moved out as soon as possible."

My curiosity as to how she had come by this distortion of what had really happened temporarily over-rode my coming clean. I said, "Did your mother call you?"

"No, Agnes did. It was maybe an hour or so before you got home. She said she'd been up the valley quilting and stopped in at the folks' place on her way home to see if mom could work this Saturday. She said Sam Cooper and his boys were there and Herb Whitworth and, oh I don't recall who else she said but I guess it was a busy place. I was thinking I would try and get off work tomorrow and go out and help them. I don't suppose you could come, could you?"

Ellen's mother worked part-time at the general store in Cedarville. It made some sense to me that Agnes Hough, who owned the store along with her husband, Ralph, would call Ellen from one of the few phones in the Gros Ventre valley and tell her what was going on with her parents. I was now anxious to set the record straight as Ellen and I had always been totally honest with one another. I was about to begin when the dinger on the oven went off. Ellen glanced back at me as she went to get my cheeseburger. "You want ketchup?"

Normally, I would say something smart-alecky like, *is the pope Catholic*? But tonight, I said only, "Yes, please."

Moments later, Ellen set the food and ketchup on the table and took a seat across from me. Before I could speak, she said, "You know Andy, I don't know what I was thinking. You wouldn't be much help moving with that bad leg."

And then I just spit the words out like they tasted bad, "I couldn't go anyway. Stroud has forbidden me from being on his property."

"What? Why's that?"

"Because I'm the reason your folks are having to move."

"You are?"

"Yeah, Stroud came upon your dad and me talking on the road this morning and well, one thing led to another and he got it in his head that your dad spilled the beans about this Garmendia guy putting out the set gun that killed Teddy Bolander. So, he blew up and fired your dad and told him to be out by noon tomorrow and told me I wasn't to set foot on his property."

The look of compassion that had been on Ellen's face just seconds ago was gone. In its place was a coldness, almost an indifference. She said, "I wished you would've left my dad out of this."

"I tried to but we just happened to run into one another there on 29. So, what am I supposed to do, not stop?"

Ellen frowned. "I don't know, Andy. It's just that my parents are too old to have this happening to them. They've lived in that house most of their adult lives and now to be kicked out, it's not right."

"Well, that's Orville Stroud for you."

Ellen's eyes had become watery as she shook her head. She said, "This isn't the first time that your job has caused this family grief."

I felt myself bow up a little. "It's what I do, Ellen."

Tears began to spill down her cheeks. She said, "I know, but sometimes I just wonder if it's worth it."

My words escaped taking with them the sentiment that I too often felt, "I can't say that I disagree with you but I've got seven more years until I can retire."

Ellen came back, her tone bitter, "A family shouldn't have to put up with what we do for 30 years to get the pitiful pension that Gros Ventre county will give you."

I said, in mock seriousness, "Well, I guess 21 years ago you should have looked a little closer at my resume. Maybe you should have kept on shopping."

Through her tears, Ellen smiled and extended her hand across the table. "No, I know a good deal when I see one."

I took her hand and squeezed it, I said, "I love you."

She whispered, "I love you too."

But in this moment of healing my mind was invaded by the image of me going out to Fred Bolander's place tomorrow morning and arresting him in front of his family. I had a bad feeling that the repercussions of this would go beyond, as Myron put it, being dropped from people's Christmas card lists.

CHAPTER EIGHT

I'd been laying on my side, most all night it seemed, staring at the dull light behind the numbers of the clock radio on the nightstand next to the bed. It read, 4:37. Around two o'clock, I'd been tempted to turn it on real low. Maybe listen to rock music from, *50,000 watts of power, KOMA, Oklahoma City.* At night it came in good, but Ellen was spooned against my back, her breathing soft and steady. So, I lay there listening to the rhythm of it and occasionally becoming fearful when the thought of not having her there entered my mind. I watched too the second hand going round and round. I pondered, if God gave a person the power to stop the second hand, to stop time, what would be the consequences of that? If somebody had done that before all this business with Stroud's herders and Teddy, would it have changed anything? I guess its human nature to rehash things you can't change. And to do it over and over, like if you do it enough times there will be some clarity come of it that allows you to see things in a way that eases your conscience. At 4:45, just as Joe Garmendia started to choke me while screaming into my face for the umpteenth time, I said to myself, *this is bullshit,* and gently rolled away from Ellen and got out of bed. I put on my bathrobe, which was lying on a cedar chest at the foot of our bed, and quietly padded out of the room to the kitchen. Ellen had put the water and coffee in our old Sunbeam percolator before going to bed last night so all I had to do was turn it on. I sat down with my elbows on the kitchen table and my forehead resting against my fingertips as I massaged that area in hopes of ridding myself of a headache that was likely caused by what I had to do today. Within a few minutes, coffee began to pulse up into the glass knob on the lid of the pot. I sat there watching its rhythmic surges and dreading what lay ahead of me. Finally, the pulses became rapid and dark and I could smell it.

"You're up early."

I'd not quite twisted around on my chair when I felt Ellen's hands on my shoulders as she gently kissed the top of my head. She added, "Couldn't you sleep?"

My first impulse was to come back at her in a loud voice, *are you kidding me? I killed a man yesterday*. But I said in a calm, almost sleepy voice, "It was kind of a long night."

She said, "I'm sorry, "and then walked over to the counter where the coffee pot was before turning around in her blue robe with its pink flowers, "You ready for a cup?"

"That'd be good."

Moments later she came back and handed me my usual coffee mug. It was red with white letters that read: World's Best Dad. I said, "Thanks, Hon, I'm movin' kinda slow this morning."

A sudden smile came to her face. "I'd say you're entitled after what happened yesterday. In fact, I wish you'd ride out to the Gros Ventre with me. It sounds like my folks have got plenty of help, so we'll just go lend a little moral support, see where it is they're moving to, and maybe have an early supper at the Lumberjack. You need a rest day."

I sighed. "I can't tell you how much I'd like to ride along with you, but I can't."

"For land sakes, Andy, you were nearly killed yesterday. You'd think the damned county would let you take today off."

"Well, there was a little more to yesterday than what I told you."

A concerned look came to her face. She said with a hint of sarcasm, "How could there be? Yesterday was bad enough."

"You'd think so, but I've been ordered by Ed Peck to arrest Fred this morning."

"You know Teddy's funeral is tomorrow morning at 11:00."

"I know, Ellen, and I know you figured we'd attend but now we, or at least me, won't be real welcome there."

Ellen took a sip of her coffee and shook her head. "Can't this wait until after the funeral. At least give the man a chance to say goodbye to his son."

"I don't have a choice. Stroud is prodding Peck to do this and he won't back down. Says he'll call Helena if I don't arrest Fred today."

Ellen scoffed and looked away as if to bleed off some of the anger that had suddenly surfaced in her face, but then she came back to me, she said, her words dripping with sarcasm, "Now, tell me again why it is you want to be the Sheriff of Gros Ventre county?"

I stood up, leaving my coffee on the table. I said, I guess I better get ready for work."

Regret came to Ellen's eyes. "But it's barely five o'clock."

"I've got lots of paperwork so I might as well get after it."

"No, Andy, I'm sorry it's just I –"

"I know Ellen, I know."

By the time I had shaved and gotten dressed Ellen had made me bacon and eggs and toast. It came with apologies to one another for how things were and then I ate another meal that I didn't particularly want. Still in her bathrobe, Ellen walked me out to my pickup. We'd speculated at length over breakfast what might be the consequences of today. There was nothing more in that regard to say. She hugged me and buried her face in my chest, just to the right of my sheriff's badge. I hugged her back, real tight. For a little bit we stood there, holding one another in the silence of the morning.

It was 5:57, just getting light. In the distance I could hear the airy, rushing sound of a car on the highway as it sped toward town. Up close, a robin was hopping around on our front lawn, pecking at insects. Other birds, it seemed, were content to sing. And then I said, with my arms still firmly wrapped around Ellen, "I better go." She'd leaned back to respond when the front door of the house opened, and Roy came out. He was barefoot, wearing gray gym shorts and a burnt orange tee shirt with black lettering on the front that read: Fremont Buccaneers. He came to the end of the sidewalk and the metal garden gate across from my truck and stopped. He said, looking at me, "Did you get called out?"

I said, with Ellen still leaning against my chest, "No, I just got things to do."

He seemed unsatisfied with my answer. "Well, it's pretty early."

I did not want to get into any of why I was going into work now or what I had to do so I put it back on Roy to explain himself. "I didn't get a chance to ask you last night but, what did you decide about your job?"

He shrugged and made a sour face. "Well, I told my boss that today will most likely be my last day."

Ellen drew away to where she could look at both Roy and me. She worked in the same office that Roy worked out of to fight fires. She said, "We'll hold Roy's resignation papers until we see if he passes his physical."

Roy laughed. "There you go again, mom, with that wishful thinking."

I said, "Did you ever call the Air Force recruiter?"

Roy shook his head. "No, I'm gonna wait until I see how the physical turns out."

I frowned. "Well, I'm not sure how these things work, but it might be too late if you wait until you've taken the physical."

"No, I talked to this guy on the crew. He said his brother did that and ended up joining the Navy."

Ellen's voice was filled with worry, she said, "Roy, you need to take this seriously. War cost both your uncles their lives."

The words escaped Roy's lips before he had a chance to think better of it. "Uncle Melvin did it to himself."

I glared at Roy and raised my voice. "C'mon Roy, you know better than that."

He came back, "I'm sorry." And then he quickly added as he started back up the sidewalk, "I'm gonna get ready for work."

I said, as the door to the house slammed behind Roy, "You know, he is trying to make the best of this."

Ellen nodded. "I know, but I sometimes think he just tells me what he thinks I want to hear."

"It's his life."

Ellen looked up at me. "Is it, Andy? Is it just his life? Doesn't he have an obligation to us to be careful with it? We're the ones that gave him life."

"There might be some preachers that would disagree with you on that."

Ellen shook her head slightly. "I know you feel what I'm saying."

"I do, but the government says he's old enough to risk his life fighting fire and now they're saying he's old enough to risk it for his country."

Tears had pooled up in her eyes. She said, "Why should we care about Vietnam? What's it to us?"

"They say we've got to go there so we can stop the spread of communism."

Ellen began to cry. I pulled her next to me. Her emotions quickly went to the point she was sobbing. I said, "We're in the same boat as thousands of other parents."

Her sobbing abruptly stopped as she stepped back and looked at me. She said sarcastically, "Do you suppose the government has let Willie Elkins' folks get out of that boat?"

I could see the fear in Ellen's face. I sensed that part of her was reliving the pain of her brothers' deaths. I felt helpless to tell her anything that would ease her anguish. Whatever I might say would likely be more, *wishful thinking*. And then she broke the impasse between us. She said, "You'd better go to work."

"And you, are you going to your folks'?"

"Yes, I'll be home by supper time."

"Be careful."

"You too." And with that she reached over and gave my hand a quick squeeze before going in the house.

As I drove out to the highway that led to town I cursed, even more, the fact that I had to do what I had to do today.

Tyler had left right after he came in for the north end of the county. That left just me and Millie in the office until it was time to go get the warrant for Fred's arrest. Silence, it turns out, can be a strong purgative as I surprised myself by laying out to her everything, in some detail, that had happened yesterday. Granted, she started this outpouring with a simple, *So, how ya doing this morning, Andy?* Her tone had been motherly, like she really cared, and just like a dirt dam crumbling, I put it out there for her to judge, for her to tell me that I'd done the right thing, and for her to tell me that, *sure, a man gets jumped from behind like that bad things are bound to happen.* I needed someone to validate my actions yesterday, both as a man and as the sheriff. It didn't quite turn out that way, but it was close enough.

Gros Ventre county has always been semi-destitute. The sheriff's office was old, having been constructed long before I was born. Conversely, the courthouse, a two-story red brick structure on the other side of town had been built about 15 years ago. At the time it was being planned I was a deputy with no say in such things, but I'd been told we'd have to make do with the current sheriff's office. There were huge cottonwood trees that lined the street in front of the courthouse. They were probably 70 to 80 years old, having been planted by the owner of the house that had been demolished to make room for the new county building. I parallel parked in the shade of the big trees and followed the sidewalk through the green oasis that surrounded the county's center for all things legal. Ed Peck's office was on the second floor near the end of the hall next to the courtroom. My footsteps echoed as I walked down the green tiled corridor past dark wood-stained doors with frosted glass top halves until I came to one labeled District Attorney. Angie Gooch, Peck's secretary, an attractive red-headed woman in her 20's was seated behind a gray metal desk that was piled high with papers and a black phone. To her right, on a pull-out table, was a typewriter. Beyond her was the door to Peck's office. As soon as she looked up, I could tell that she knew all about yesterday. Her expression suddenly went from being calm to almost flustered. She immediately stood and said in a reserved tone, "I'll tell Mr. Peck you're here." This was from a woman that I'd known for over five years and talked to almost weekly.

I said, purposely shedding light on her personal indifference to me, "Alright, thanks Angie."

She gave me an uncomfortable glance before disappearing into Peck's office. Their voices were muffled and went on long enough to make me suspicious of what was going on until the door abruptly opened and Angie came out closing the door behind her. She handed me the arrest warrant and said, "Mr. Peck wants you to call after you've served this."

I thought it odd that Peck wouldn't come out of his office and deal with this personally since he'd made such a big deal about it, but I said simply, "Ok," and stepped out into the hall. The warrant had been folded in thirds and placed in a long envelope which usually wasn't the case. I'd taken four or five slow steps by the time I got the envelope open and the paper unfolded. My eyes glossed over the boiler plate coming to a halt on the line where the alleged crime was indicated: MITIGATED DELIBERATE HOMICIDE. The words stopped me in my tracks. This was a serious charge, much more than what I thought Fred deserved. I stood there, staring at the warrant, re-reading it just to be sure. I had two choices. I could be an obedient civil servant and go serve Fred with the warrant and bring him in, or I could go back inside and argue with Peck to amend the charge. I chose the latter. I was just opening the door when I heard Peck say to Angie, "What'd he say?"

I cut in, "I'll tell ya what I've got to say. This is crap. Fred's run-in with that sheep herder is aggravated assault, at most."

Being on his own turf there in the courthouse, Peck came back quick and angry. "That's not your call."

"You know it was a fight that just got out of hand."

"Yeah, a fight that Bolander started. That herder was minding his own business until Bolander attacked him."

"Oh, for hell sakes, Peck, he was upset. Show a little compassion, the man had his dead son in the back of his pickup. Why, he could get 40 years for this? You think that's right?"

"Well, that's 40 more years than Felipe Arriola has."

"This will ruin Fred's family."

"He should've thought of that before he attacked that herder"

"He was distraught, Ed. The exit wound in his kid's back was the size of a saucer."

From the corner of my eye I could see Angie grimace before getting up and going out into the hall. I said, "C' mon Ed, do the right thing here. Amend the charge to aggravated assault."

"I'd have to take it back to the judge."

"He's just across the hall."

"Stroud would pitch a fit."

I snorted, "Who gives a shit what Stroud thinks? He's the one that started all this by having Garmendia put out that set gun."

"He swears up and down that if Garmendia put a gun out, it was on his own."

"And you believe that?"

Peck went quiet for a second like he was collecting his anger and then he said, "We're done arguing this. Go bring your friend in. He'll have his day in court."

I looked back at Peck with as much hate as I could muster and said, "Yeah, he will and he'll have to hire some damned three piece suit to speak for him and when it's all said and done he'll have to sell all of his cattle, or his ranch, or both, to keep from spending the rest of his life in Deerlodge."

Peck shook his head in a contemptuous manner and then looked hard at me, "We're done here, Sheriff. Now get the hell out of my office."

It was difficult to contain my anger, but I could see it was best I leave now. There would be no changing Peck's mind. I glared at him one last time and then went out the door, not succumbing to the temptation to slam it. I stopped abruptly. To my left, seated on a honey oak bench along the wall was Angie. She stood up and whispered, "You should be careful of what you say, Andy."

My inner voice said sarcastically, *Oh, so now you know my name.* I said aloud, "This is overkill."

Angie looked over at the door and then back at me, she said, keeping her voice low, "I heard them talking."

"Who?"

"Peck and Judge Barela. They're concerned that there's no witnesses to the fight and that if Mr. Bolander claims the herder threw the first punch it could come down to self-defense."

"So, they're over charging him hoping that he'll plead to something lesser."

Angie nodded. "They're convinced, or rather Orville Stroud has convinced them, that Bolander threw the first punch."

I thought back to what Fred had told me at the funeral home. It dealt mostly with finding Teddy and the set gun. At this point, I couldn't dispute Fred if he was to say the herder started the fight. Notable gossip travels fast in a small town, so he likely now knew the herder had died and that he was in trouble. If he was smart, he'd be putting together a story that was favorable to him staying out of prison. The truth as to what actually happened might become a casualty. I said. "I can't say one way or another."

Angie's eyes suddenly became alarmed and shifted to the door behind me, I looked back. Silhouetted through the frosted glass was Peck's outline. Angie raised her voice, "It was good talking to you, Andy. Tell Ellen I said hello."

I glanced back at Peck's shadow again and smiled. I said loud enough that he could hear, "I'll do that. She mentions every now and again what fun it was having you work summers for the forest service."

Angie came back, smiling as she completed our little melodrama for Peck's benefit, "Yes, I really enjoyed working there, but not as much as I do here."

I almost laughed before saying a little louder than necessary, "Well, I better get on down the road." We both watched and smiled as Peck's outline quickly evaporated.

Angie whispered, "Be careful today."

I nodded and walked away.

CHAPTER NINE

It occurred to me as I left the city limits that here I was going out to serve a felony arrest warrant by myself. But overshadowing this caution was the image that always came to my mind whenever I thought of Fred Bolander. It wasn't of the man with bloodstained clothes and bruised knuckles who I'd seen a few days ago at the funeral home, but rather it was shy little Freddy Bolander in his blue and gold Future Farmers of America jacket. I knew, of course, that people weren't always what they appeared to be. Take for instance last fall when Jim Simmons, Roy's little league coach, fled a game department check station at the edge of town because he had an untagged deer. I was called, as was a Fremont City officer, to chase Simmons down. A high speed pursuit through the streets of Fremont ensued before a game warden was able to block the street with his pickup causing our little league coach to bail out of his truck with a cocked .357 magnum screaming, *You sorry sons-a-bitches better back off.* He was another person that day. It ultimately led to him getting shot, spending time in the hospital and the state penitentiary at Deerlodge. I hoped today that the Fred Bolander who had beaten Felipe Arriola to death wasn't home, but the little Freddy of 25 years ago was.

To either side of the highway were fields of hay that had been mostly cut and baled, grain that was being combined, and irrigated pasture that was populated with red and black cows. Interspersed in all of this were ranch houses, out buildings, corrals and lots of haystacks. In the distance beyond the fields were timber covered mountains. Up ahead on the left was a T intersection. A gray wooden post stood on the far side of it. Nailed to it were a series of white boards with black lettering about four inches high by a foot and a half wide. They read like a menu column beginning with the fact this was the Elk Creek Road, below this were the ranches located up it. There were eight placards on the post. The fifth one down read: Bolander's Broken Heart Ranch – 5 miles. To the right of this they'd applied their brand; two halves of a heart, slightly offset with a quarter circle beneath the two. I shifted down and turned onto the gravel road and sped up to about 35. It was a nice sunny day, not a cloud in the sky. Here I was driving along with my arm out the window listening to the radio like I was going fishing or something. Off to my right in a lush green pasture that the cows had not yet taken down to golf course standards was a herd of about 15 or 20 antelope. They barely noticed my driving by, but in another half mile or so I came upon a fellow cutting hay. He was perched on an old lime green Owatonna swather watching its gaudy red paddle reel pull the hay down simultaneous to it being severed and spewed out behind in a nice, neat windrow. The machine had seen better days. Its noisy motor sat right next to the driver's seat. The man, who I recognized as Bill Nichols, was hunched forward with his hands on the steering levers staring intently ahead. But then he detected the movement of my pickup coming up the road. He was a good hundred yards out into the field. At first glance he was like the antelope but then, I suppose, his mind processed the big gold badge on the door of my truck, and he looked straight at me. He did not wave, just kept looking until I was on by him. In my mind, I could hear him in his old gravelly voice saying, *there goes the damned law to haul Fred in.* It caused the naysayer in my mind to throw me a surprise pity party. *Yeah, you're a great guy when they need you, but on down the road you're a S.O.B..* I sighed and looked out the window just as a fish took a fly off the surface of some slow deep water in the bend of the creek. It momentarily made me wish that I worked for Jake's Feed & Seed, or some such place, and that today was my day off and I was going fishing. Hell, I'd settle for just being able to go with Ellen out to the Gros Ventre today to help her folks move. And so it went, my mind spinning nothing good until I came around a blind curve in the road owing to the aspen and willows along the creek and there was Fred's pale yellow clapboard house set off beneath some big cottonwood trees. I turned at their mailbox, which was a miniature red barn with a black roof sitting on top of a wooden post. On the side of it in white letters was simply, BOLANDER. I drove past it and across the bridge towards their house. A barn that resembled the mailbox was set off to the left. There was a pole corral attached to it and back to the east of this was a pale blue metal grainary, a horse trailer, a John Deere tractor and baler, a two-bottom tumble-bug plow, a GMC truck and lots of other stuff. Some of it was functional and some not, but at one time or another it had been needed to operate the ranch. No one was in sight but then Teddy's dog, Bosco, came running out, like he did everybody I suppose, to greet me. Fred's pickup was parked in front of a hog wire fence stapled to wooden posts that surrounded the grass around the house. A red Chevy station wagon was parked next to it. I'd barely gotten out of my pickup when the door to the house opened and out came the Bolanders, Fred, his wife Norma and their son Owen, who I'd heard was on leave from the Army. Fred came as far as the gate in the fence and then stopped. I could tell by his eyes that he knew why I was there. He said, "I was hoping to not see you until after tomorrow."

"Well Fred, that would've been my druthers too but sometimes things just don't work out like you want."

Owen, who stood a head taller than his father and probably 30 pounds heavier, stepped up to the fence. "Well, you're the sheriff aren't ya? Don't you call the shots?"

I could see that the boy's makeup favored his mother. He had dark brown hair, cut Army short, and green eyes. A pack of Camel cigarettes was rolled up in the right sleeve of his white tee shirt. Beneath it was what appeared to be a tattoo of the word: AIRBORNE. Before I could answer him, Norma said, "You don't have to do this, Andy, not today you don't."

I said, looking at all of them, "I'm sorry, it can't be helped."

Owen jumped in, "Well, if you ask me this is pretty chickenshit. My dad was just defending himself against the fella that killed Teddy and now you want to put him in jail before Teddy's even in the ground. I'll tell ya, if you wasn't wearing that badge I'd throw your ass in the crik." And then he added, "Maybe with some rocks tied to it."

Fred turned to his son. He said angrily, "That's enough." And then he added, "threatening him will just make it worse."

Out of the blue, Norma looked hard at me and seethed the words, "You're a despicable shit, Andy Yarnell. You'd be well advised to not forget that what goes around comes around."

I looked at Norma and considered for a moment apologizing, but then I turned to Fred, "We should probably go."

Owen came to life, "Hold on there, I know enough that you can't be hauling somebody off because it suits you. Ain't you supposed to have a warrant?"

I reached in my back pocket and pulled out the envelope. "Got it right here."

Fred said, "Can I read it? I'd like to know how that fat little toad of a district attorney sees this."

I tried to keep my face in a neutral place as I opened the envelope. A gentle gust of wind caused the paper to flutter as I handed it to Fred. Within a few seconds, his reaction was not too much unlike mine the first time I had read it, he said, "What the hell is this Mitigated Deliberate Homicide? Sounds serious to me."

I suddenly felt like I was about to lose control of the situation. Nonetheless, I did not try to deceive Fred. I said, "It is, they can send you to Deerlodge for a long time if you're found guilty."

Fred snorted and looked at me like I was an idiot. "Whaddaya mean, if I'm found guilty? There's no question that sheepherder and me got in a fight."

I glanced down at Fred's bruised knuckles. There were a couple of soft scabs on his right hand most likely the result of cuts he got when his fist knocked in Arriola's front teeth. I said, "The question, Fred, will be who threw the first punch?

Fred went quiet. He didn't immediately shout out, *why, that guy did!* Instead, I could see it in his eyes that he was back out there on Porphyry Creek. Finally, after too much time had passed for him to have any credibility, he said, "That fella wouldn't move his sheep off the road so I honked my horn and it made some of the sheep scatter, but I still couldn't get through. Hell, there musta been close to a thousand of 'em all piled onto the road next to the crik."

I said, in a voice as if we were sitting in the Lumberjack drinking coffee and telling stories, "Probably lettin' 'em water 'fore he pushed up on the side of the mountain."

Fred became defensive, "Maybe he was, but he just sat there on his horse like we both had nothing but time. I was in a hurry to get Teddy back to town."

As much as I didn't want it to, my internal bullshit alarm went off, I said, "This is kinda peculiar, Fred. Most generally, a herder is Johnny-on-the-spot with ridin' ahead of you to clear a path.' I hesitated but regrettably added, "I think they've learned the hard way it's best to do this if they don't want an animal's hind legs colliding with a car bumper."

Fred gave me a dirty look like I took him for some town person that didn't know up from down about how livestock behave. He said, "I got out of my pickup and hollered at the guy and he waved his arm at me and yelled something in Spanish or basco talk or whatever it is they speak and started my way."

"Well, at this point, where was he from you?"

"He was across the crik."

"Oh, so he was some distance away?"

"Yeah, but Andy, you know that crik and the road right next to it. Hell, I can spit across Porphyry Crik."

I nodded, "So, Arriola crosses the creek on horseback and comes over to you? I guess he must have got down for you two to get in a fight."

Fred came back, his voice kind of lost, searching too long for the words, "Yeah, he did. He splashed right through the crik. I could tell he was purty full of himself."

I cut in, "Was he saying anything?"

I'd caught Fred off-guard. "Oh, uh, yeah he was, but like I said I don't understand his lingo. He was mad as a wet hen and you can take that to the bank."

"And so, after he gets off his horse what'd he do? Did he say something or did he just come at you?"

"Well, he pointed at my pickup and started off on some rant that I couldn't understand and then the next thing I know he's right up in my face screaming at me. I told him he better step back or there'd be trouble, but then he just up and shoves me. I fell against the hood of my pickup and before I know it, he was on me, throwin' punches."

In my twenty plus years of being a lawman I'd met some pretty accomplished liars, but Fred wasn't one of them. And even though he saw that I was looking at the damage to his hands, he made no attempt to hide them. I figured any obligation I had to explain myself to Fred and his family had been satisfied by having just participated in the charade of facts that Fred had just manufactured. Armed with the information that I'd been given at the courthouse this morning, I said, "Fred, I'd suggest you get yourself a lawyer and see what kind of a deal you can strike with the district attorney."

Owen said sarcastically, "Those sons-ah-bitches ain't cheap, ya know."

I looked beyond Fred to Owen who was now lighting a cigarette. I said, "I don't see where your pa has much choice."

Owen exhaled a cloud of blue smoke in front of his face. He said, talking before the smoke was completely out of his lungs, "Oh, he probably doesn't and that's the worst part of this deal. A man can't just speak for himself."

I cut in, "He can, but I wouldn't recommend it."

Owen laughed at me like I was some kind of fool. He came back, "So, we're supposed to run into town and hire some pencil neck in a suit to cut a deal?"

Fred said, "When do you think I can make this deal?"

I grinned slightly and tossed my head back. "This ain't no traffic ticket, Fred. You've got to be arraigned and bail set and so on. It's gonna be awhile before you get to any deal making. You just need to get yourself a lawyer."

Norma scoffed, "The only lawyer I know of in Fremont is that old Herb Boyer and he's a shyster from what I hear."

Fred said, "What about him, Andy? You think Boyer would do for this?"

I was hesitant to give any more legal advice than I already had but I'd opened this can of worms. I said, "Well, he mostly does wills and divorces but he has over the years defended a few people in criminal matters."

"So, how'd things turn out for those folks?"

"Oh, about fifty-fifty, I guess."

"Were they guilty?"

I nodded. "Near as I could tell, they were."

Fred gave a long, worried sigh and then turned to Norma, he said, "Well, Hon, I guess after you're done at O'Leary's you better run by Boyer's office and see if you can hire him on. Make sure to take the check book with you."

Norma squinted her eyes in an effort to hold back the tears and shook her head. "This is just not right, Fred. I can't do this alone."

At that moment, Owen was spewing cigarette smoke. It shrouded his face and his reaction to his mother feeling that she was all alone.

Fred stood there, in his yard, just on the other side of his fence. The anger in his eyes had been replaced with fear, maybe because the awareness that he was no longer a free man had set in. He couldn't do something as simple as go back to his house with his family and have a cold glass of tea on the front porch and look at the blue sky and sunshine and remark, *It's a fine day, isn't it*. He said to me, "I guess it's time to go, huh?"

I said, as I nodded and reached for the handcuffs on my belt. "Yeah, it is."

Fred said, "Hell, Andy, I ain't no desperado. You think I aim to give you trouble?"

Norma broke into a loud sobbing cry.

Owen threw in, "He's cuffin' ya, Pa, cuz he's afraid of ya."

I glared at Owen. "It's standard procedure."

Owen snorted, "My ass it is."

Fred turned his head slightly as he threw the words over his shoulder, his tone was sharp, "Let it go, Owen."

I looked at Fred and said with a tone of reluctance in my voice, "I need for you to hold your hands out."

Fred eyed the cuffs for a few seconds before extending his hands towards me. As I closed them on his wrists, Norma regained her composure sufficient to say, "How do you live with yourself, Andy? This ain't right what you're doing."

I looked briefly at Norma, as if I owed her that courtesy while she insulted me, and then I came back to Fred. "It's time to go."

Fred turned to Norma, he said, "It'll be all right, you'll see."

Norma had gone back to crying full time as she stepped close to Fred and hugged him like he was an armless person. She hung on beyond what might be a normal hug until Fred said, "I better go."

Norma separated herself just barely from Fred. Tears were cascading down her cheeks and her nose had released a torrent of snot that was channeling to the sides of her thick upper lip. She whispered, "I love you."

Fred said, "I love you too," and then he kissed her lightly on the lips.

As the emotions between his parents played out, Owen seemed content to smoke his Camel and watch my reaction to what I was causing. The expression on his face looked to be just short of evil. Fred had stepped through the gate and was walking slightly in front of me towards my pickup when from behind us Owen shouted, "When can we come visit?"

I turned to face him. Right off, I sensed in his eyes he was setting me up for something else, I said, "Your pa will be at the city/county facility. Visiting hours there are seven to eight tonight."

Owen frowned. "Well, that's just fine and dandy. We gotta be at the undertakers at one-thirty to make final arrangements for Teddy, so then if we wanna see Pa we gotta wait around till seven o'clock tonight.'

I said, "Sorry, I don't set their hours."

"Well, why don't you put him in your jail?"

I had a feeling where he was going with this but I had no choice but to go along. I said, "It's only for temporary holding."

A sarcastic, smug grin came over his face, he said, "Well, that's real handy. You get to go home at five o'clock, put up your feet, open a beer and watch the news while that missus of yours fixes you supper."

Regrettably, I did not keep walking, I said, "You don't know what you're talking about."

"Well, I do believe that the sheriff's office does close at five and I know for a fact that you're married to one of them Orientals and they're known for waitin' on their men folk."

I shook my head in disgust and turned away. "Let's go, Fred."

I knew it must have been hard for Fred to walk away from his crying wife, but maybe less so from the antagonistic talk of his son. To his credit, he did not hesitate to open the passenger door of my truck and climb in. The freedom of movement that he, and probably Owen and Norma too, thought he would have vanished as I picked up a chain that was attached to an eyebolt in the floor and hooked it onto the chain between his cuffs. It made it so Fred couldn't raise his hands off of his lap and I didn't need to worry about him having a change of heart on the way back to town. I backed around and started slowly out of the yard with Bosco in pursuit, barking until we reached the bridge and rattled the one loose plank in it before turning onto the road and picking up speed. For a good while we rode without talking, pretending to listen to the radio above the rushing air outside the open windows. It wasn't until we had been on 29 for a while and getting close to town that a song called, *Hello Vietnam* by Johnnie Wright came on the radio. Fred allowed it to play out and a commercial for a sale on tires at some place in Great Falls had come on before he said, "I don't know if that fella's song has got it right."

For a few seconds his words did not penetrate the hodge-podge of thoughts in my head but then some of its lyrics floated to the top, *Kiss me goodbye and write me while I'm gone...*, I said, "How do ya mean, Fred?"

"Owen says we're pissin' in the wind over there."

I sighed as I glanced over at him, "I can't say. It does seem to be a helluva price we're payin though."

Fred nodded. "Yeah, it sure does. I can tell ya, the Owen that went over there isn't the Owen that came back."

From the corner of my eye, I could see that Fred was studying my face to see, I suppose, if I'd gotten the meaning of what he'd said. Before I could say anything, he double downed, "He really isn't a bad kid. This morning just wasn't a good deal for us."

I said, "I know, Fred. I know."

CHAPTER TEN

It was a few minutes past noon when I pulled into the gravel parking lot behind the courthouse. The city/county jail and 24-hour dispatch were located in its basement. I felt sorry for Fred. Here he was a respectable rancher until day before yesterday and now he was having his picture taken, being fingerprinted, stripped of his clothing and made to wear orange coveralls with the words, GROS VENTRE COUNTY PRISONER stenciled in bold black letters on the back. The jail complex could hold a maximum of 15 inmates, Fred made number fourteen. The cells were arranged in an L shape. Eight were located down a hall straight out from the booking area, with seven more around the corner in another hallway. The jailor, a heavy-set middle-aged woman with short blonde hair whose name was Beatrice, but went by Bee, allowed me to tag along as she took Fred back to his cell. We'd just turned the corner into the next hallway when I noted all of the prisoners were eating. I said to Bee, "So, what's for lunch?"

She said, with a hint of indifference, "White bread peanut butter sandwich, some potato chips and a cup of water."

Fred said, "I don't recall the last time I had a peanut butter sandwich."

Bee came back with a dose of sarcasm, "Well, today is your lucky day."

I shot a brief scowl at Fred as if to say, *you don't want to be pissin' her off.*

Fred remained quiet for approximately the next 30 feet until Bee stopped at a cell whose door was slightly ajar. She opened it and gestured to him. "Alright, sweetheart, here ya are."

Fred hesitated, like he had a choice, and looked inside. To his right was a narrow bunk with a mattress about three inches thick and two green blankets that appeared to be Army surplus. Near the head of the bed along the wall was a stainless-steel toilet and sink. A shelf about a foot wide by three inches deep protruded from the wall above the sink. In the ceiling directly overhead was a light bulb and, just like the ones out in the hall, it was encased in heavy wire mesh. It was turned off at 9:00 P.M. but those in the hallway stayed on all the time as there were no windows anywhere. The cinderblock walls were a pale yellow while the floor had the same green tile as the courthouse. At last Bee said in a heavy mocking tone, "Excuse me sir, this, *is,* your room."

A helpless look came over Fred's face as he stared a hole through Bee towards me. I said, not knowing what else to say at that moment, "It's Friday, Fred. You may not get an arraignment until Monday. So, you'll have to sit tight. Maybe Norma can bring you something to read tonight."

Fred's expression graduated to angry disbelief but before he could verbalize this, the hippy in the cell next to him began retching loudly. He could be heard clearly above the constant din of the other prisoner's incessant banter. Bee stepped over to where she could look into his cell. She instantly went off, "You sonovabitch. At least you could've puked in the toilet."

I looked over Bee's shoulder. The hippy had been laying on his bed, but now he was on his hands and knees on the floor. A trail of vomit led from the bed to the floor. Even his orange coveralls were stained. The stench of warm puke permeated the air. Bee glared at the hippy as he strained to bring up the last of his stomach contents. She shook her head angrily but then stepped back in front of Fred's cell, she said, "I'll be back in a minute with your lunch."

Fred laughed derisively, "Lady, you've got a stronger stomach than I do."

Bee snorted. "Fine, but don't be bitchin' about being hungry later." And with that she started up the hall.

I looked at Fred standing there in his cell. Even after all these years of being in law enforcement the stark contrast of a jail cell bothered me, it was a place I never wanted to be. I said, "You'll be alright, Fred. One day at a time." It may have been that he picked out the uncertainty in my voice, but he just shrugged and sat down on his bed. I walked away.

Although I'd been to the jail complex countless times over the years, today was different. I was anxious to leave, to separate myself from the constant, seemingly unnecessary, echoing racket of the prisoners who respected no one's privacy because there was none. It may have been too that I saw some of myself in Fred. If it had been Roy who had stumbled into that set gun, I might have done the same thing as Fred. And Owen, he had been a year ahead of Roy in school, a good athlete, respectful as I recall. But now, the school boy in him was gone. I wondered if this was how Roy would be if he went to Vietnam. I was about to knock on the small plexiglass window to let the guard know I wanted out, when the door opened. The odor of ammonia was strong and immediate. I stepped to the side as Bee wheeled a heavy metal mop bucket past me. She barely acknowledged that I was there as she mumbled over the squeak of the bucket's wheels, "Oughta make that damned hippy clean up his own puke."

I caught the door before it closed and locked again, but paused midway through it when one of the prisoners shouted as Bee rolled by, "Oh, housekeeping, could you clean my room too. Some fresh towels would be nice." And then the man started laughing as did his neighbors to either side.

Bee shot back, "Just keep it up smartass and see what you get for supper."

The man came to the bars and looked at Bee as she squeaked on down the hall, he shouted, "What, no prime rib tonight?" And then he and his friends laughed some more. Oddly, in that very instant I found myself sympathizing with the prisoners. The hopeless boredom of the cell block was crushing. To laugh at anyone's expense was a treat. Bee, knowing that she'd never be able to get the best of the man, kept quiet and rounded the corner.

As I limped across the parking lot to my pickup, it occurred to me that I had done as Peck and Stroud had wanted and that my nose, a couple of my teeth and my calf where I'd been stabbed all were throbbing with pain. By the time I reached my truck I knew what I was going to do. I reached for my radio's mic but stopped short, thinking, *there ain't no point in advertising where I'll be, I'll call Millie later.* And so, I started towards home with the intentions of having a ham sandwich and a beer in the shade of the patio. I had my windows down listening to the radio. One of my favorite Patsy Cline songs, *I Fall To Pieces*, was playing and I was well into analyzing my life. It made for a tranquil mood, far better than my morning had been. But then I pulled onto Main Street and things went south. Up ahead of me, a red '64 GTO shot out from a side street running the stop sign like he owned the road and burned rubber for a good 40 or 50 feet before getting traction and taking off only to hit 2nd gear and screech his rear wheels again.

I sighed and whispered aloud, "Oh, shit, here we go," and then I reached over and hit my lights and siren. I floored my old Ford pickup but I wasn't gaining at all on the GTO, until suddenly, a white Buick pulled out from Brewer's drive-in right in the path of the speeding car. Even though the GTO's tires screamed and shed blue smoke, it wasn't enough to keep from hitting the Buick. The GTO mostly impacted the left front portion of the Buick but it had enough force to cause the Buick's passenger side door to pop open and eject a teenage girl.

I brought my pickup to a halt just short of the GTO. A teenage boy dressed in holey faded Levis and a green tee shirt with a red, white and blue peace symbol on the front stared back at me as I called in the accident. The kid didn't fit the image of most Fremont teens. He had dark shoulder length hair and a wispy moustache. The two girls that had been riding in the Buick had drifted over to the edge of the street and were talking to a few people that had migrated from the drive-in, Emma being one of them. The girls, who were both wearing shorts and sandals, appeared to be ok other than the chubby one, a blonde, had a scrape on her right shin. From this distance it looked to be minor with a trickle of blood petering out after an inch or so. Given this, I kept on towards the driver of the GTO. The closer I got the more I absorbed his likely motivation for doing what he had. He was no different than an old Hereford bull. Brewer's drive-in was a favorite place for teenagers, especially girls, to congregate in the summer. Mr. GTO's reckless display was no coincidence. I stopped a few feet from him. He already had his license and registration in his hand suggesting this was not a new experience. His bloodshot eyes indicated he might have reason to be more nervous than what he was showing. Instead, he seemed a little on the cocky side. I purposely stopped within a few feet of him. The smell of marijuana was strong. I said, "You know what you just did could've killed people, don't you?"

There was no remorse in the kid's face, he said, "They shouldn't have pulled out in front of me."

I felt a stab of anger as I shook my head, "If you'd been going the speed limit you could've stopped in time."

"Nobody got hurt."

"I frowned in disbelief, "This time they didn't. I need to see your license and registration, please."

He held the documents out to me. I looked at the registration first and became even more angry. I had to concentrate on not allowing it to show as I read his driver's license. I said, "You're Orville Stroud's son?"

A smug look came to the kid's face. "Yeah, I am."

I said, "Well, William, you're in some serious trouble here."

He smirked, "I ran a stop sign, big deal. The wreck is those girl's fault."

"Not the way I see it. I'm citing you for running the stop sign and reckless driving and I believe you've been smoking pot so I'll be searching your car."

"You can't do that."

"Oh, yes I can. You reek of pot. Your eyes are watery and bloodshot. That's probable cause to me."

The kid smirked. "You're just hassling me cuz you've got it out for my old man. That shit ain't gonna work."

I smiled. "I guess we'll see, but for now you need to go stand in front of my pickup."

"And if I don't."

My mind, or my ego I guess, instantly went to the fight with Joe. This kid had no doubt heard about it from his father and now, did he think that he could intimidate me? I laughed and looked hard into his eyes and then said calmly, "Well, I'll handcuff you and put you in the cab of my pickup and chain your hands so you can't even swat a fly."

For a few seconds, he looked at me like he was sizing me up as to whether I could make good on what I'd just said before finally giving me another one of his shitty little grins and walking off towards my truck. I looked over at the driver of the Buick and motioned for her and her friend to come back to their car. At about this time, Virgil Moore, a city patrolman pulled up on the far side of the Buick and parked his car. It was going to be close who reached me first, Virgil or the girls, in the end the girls won. Virgil, was a young muscular guy with a military haircut. He was wearing aviator sunglasses that seemed to blend with his dark blue uniform. As he joined our group the girls suddenly got shy. Virgil glanced at me and then at Stroud's kid, he said in a sour tone, "Aren't you the lucky one?"

I wasn't certain if his sarcasm referred to my difficulties with Orville Stroud and the fact the state highway patrol were reviewing my actions leading up to my shooting Joe Garmendia, or that William Stroud was a delinquent destined for a long-term relationship with the police. I said, "You know, William?"

"Oh, yeah. We know one another quite well. I imagine he'll be walking after this."

I grinned and nodded my head. "Well, the streets will be safer if his mode of travel is restricted to a pair of tennis shoes."

The girls were still giggling as I said to the chubby one, "Are you alright?"

She glanced down at the cut on her leg before looking at me. "It's nothing. I'll put a band-aid on it when I get home."

"You're sure, cuz now's the time to say?"

"Yeah, I think so."

I turned to the driver, a tall brunette, "I need your license and registration."

"It's my parents' car."

"That's ok, I just need to see that it has a current registration and you have a driver's license."

"Oh, alright." The girls went to the passenger side of the Buick and began rummaging through the glove box.

I lowered my voice and said to Virgil. "I think William is high on pot."

"That doesn't surprise me. I've smelled it on him before, but the one time that I searched his car I came up empty. I think he must have tossed it before I got him stopped."

"Well, I told him that I was going to search his car and he got real unhappy about it."

Virgil laughed. "Have at it, I'll deal with the girls."

William's eyes were locked on to me as I walked toward the GTO. I opened the door and was immediately overwhelmed with the smell of pot. The inside of the car was a mess. There were empty chip bags, a thermos of Kool-aid, candy bar wrappers, a half-full cup of Coke from the drive-in and the wrapper from a hamburger but, as I expected, there was no pot out in plain sight. However, this didn't concern me, what did was when I found cigarette papers and some plastic baggies in the glove box but no pot, not even after looking under the front seats, behind the visors, in the trunk and under the rear seat. It was at this point that I happened to look back at William, he was grinning broadly as he shouted, "You're wasting your time." And then he laughed.

I turned away so as to not give him anymore satisfaction in seeing my frustration than he was already getting. I stood there, scanning the inside of the car while replaying in my mind the period of time from when I lit him up until he crashed into the Buick. I was certain that he hadn't thrown anything out, especially with him hot-rodding the car the way he was. But then I noticed something odd about the bottom of the thermos. It was black as was the rest of it, except for the chrome cup that screwed down over the stopper. But, on the bottom, there was small white print that said where the thermos had been made. To either side of this, near the outer edge, were shallow dimples. Their depth and spacing clicked in my mind as a way to unscrew the bottom of the thermos. I inserted my thumb in one depression and my index finger in the other and twisted. After several turns the lower third of the thermos came off. Within its hollowness was loose marijuana, by my estimate about three or four ounces, enough to get you a felony in Montana and a five year stay at Deerlodge. I held the cup up for William to see and shouted, "Well, look what I found. This isn't some of that gourmet tea is it?" I couldn't help but laugh.

William shot me a dirty look and yelled, "Screw you, pig."

The chubby Buick girl along with Emma and a few others that were still standing at the curb all looked at William in a disgusted way. As I twisted the bottom back onto the thermos and walked towards him, I could see from the corner of my eye that Emma was watching me. It caused me to look over at her. She gave me a smile and a little wave and much more, as my self- doubt of a moment ago became unimportant. I nodded to her before looking back at William. He was looking at Emma and then back at me, and then he laughed. As I neared him, he said, "So, that's your kid?"

I said simply, "Yes," as I walked past him and put the thermos in my pickup.

To my back he said, "Figures, she's a stuck-up bitch."

Anger fueled my first impulse, as over the years I'd been insulted, even spit on, enough times to know that this kid was just taking free shots at me because he knew I couldn't retaliate. Nonetheless, I spun around causing bolts of pain to shoot up my injured calf as I hobbled back to the front of my pickup. I looked at William, not mean or hateful, but rather calmly and indifferent, like he was nothing to me. I said, "Put out your hands. I'm placing you under arrest for possession of marijuana and reckless driving."

"You can't do that."

"Yes, I can. Now, put out your hands."

William scoffed and held out his hands. I put the cuff on his left wrist and was about to do the right when he suddenly jerked it away and gave the finger to the small crowd of onlookers. He yelled, "Screw you bitches."

Instantly, my left hand shot out and grabbed his raised hand and pulled it back to where I could cuff it. I said, "You need to settle down. You're not helping your cause."

He snorted indignantly. "You're wasting your time. My old man will have me out this afternoon."

"Don't count on it. According to your driver's license you turned 18 two weeks ago. So, happy birthday. You're an adult in the state of Montana in possession of enough weed and paraphernalia to be charged with intent to distribute. You're not going to just get a slap on the hands and walk out."

William scowled at me as he shook his head, but he said nothing more.

From behind me, Virgil said, "So, you're going to take our friend in?"

I glanced over at Virgil as I took hold of William's left arm and started to the passenger side of my pickup. I said, "William appears to be in the business of selling pot."

"Well, that's not good."

"No, it's not."

Virgil elevated his voice to a kind of jovial tone. "But hey, on the bright side, I hear they're having beef stew at the jail tonight. It's mighty tasty." And then he laughed.

William ignored Virgil and did his best to pretend he was unphased by my attaching the chain to his cuffs and shutting the door. I said to Virgil, "Do you mind finishing up here?"

He shook his head. "Not a problem. The Buick's drivable, so the girls can go on their way and I've got a tow truck coming for Billy boys' GTO."

"Thanks Virgil. I owe you a soda pop."

He laughed. "Yeah, or something."

Within minutes I was back at the city/county jail and standing in front of Bee with Billy in tow. I said, "got another customer for ya."

Bee looked up from behind her desk. Her appraisal of Billy was quick, his long hair, bloodshot eyes and the stench of marijuana. She said, slow and emphatic, "You've got to be shitting me. Another hippy pothead. I just got the barf cleaned up in the other one's cell and now here you come with this guy. Where are you finding these people? I thought Fremont was a respectable town."

"Honest Bee, I was trying to help you out. I was on my way home when this guy almost runs me over."

William, or Billy as Virgil knew him, gave me a dirty look. "You're a real comedian."

Bee ignored Billy's comment and sighed, "Alright, let's get you checked in."

It took about 30 minutes for Billy to complete all of the steps necessary to surrender his freedom. Included in this process was allowing him to call the Cedarville store. On any other Friday, Niko Lujack, my mother-in-law, would have answered the phone. But since Billy's father had kicked her and Phil out of the house that they'd lived in for the last 40 years, she was off today, moving. Instead, Ralph Hough, the owner had answered. Billy's insistence that he get word to his father immediately got him nowhere. Ralph had told him *I'll send word out if somebody comes in that's headed that way, but I can't go.* At this point Billy started to argue and Ralph hung up. Billy slammed the phone down, "That sonovabitch will be sorry. My dad does a lot of business there."

I said, with some satisfaction, "It's a long-ways to town just for a can of beans or sack of flour."

Before Billy could dish out something smart aleck, Bee said, "Alright, Mr. Stroud, let's go on back."

I said, not because I didn't think Bee couldn't handle Billy but more because I felt an obligation to check on Fred, "You mind if I walk along with you."

She said, in her usual hardened curt manner, "Be my guest." But then, before we'd taken only a couple of steps, she stopped and went to her desk and picked up a little magazine of crossword puzzles and a pencil and handed them to me. "You can give him this."

I nodded my appreciation.

The erosion of Billy's bravado began within seconds of our entering the cell block when a man with black hair and several days growth of whiskers called out, "Does your mama know where you're at?" He paused to laugh and then went on, "Boy, I bet you get a whippin' when you get home – if you ever do." And then he laughed again as did the men to either side of him. We moved along the gauntlet of insults turning the corner towards Billy's new home. Up ahead, a big man with wild unkempt hair and a bushy black moustache that hid his upper lip but not his yellow teeth, was leaning into the bars of the cell just before Billy's. He grinned, knowing full well the fear he could cause Billy, and said, "Well hello, Sweetheart, looks like we're going to be neighbors."

I glanced over at Billy. I could see the man had gotten the effect he desired and I thought to tell Billy, *it's just jailhouse talk, don't pay it any attention.* But then I recalled what he'd said about Emma and I kept quiet letting him stew over it.

Bee opened the door of the hippy's old cell. The odor of ammonia with just a hint of vomit was strong. She gestured for Billy to go in. "Here ya go, last bed in the house."

Billy looked at me in a hateful way making sure our eyes met. He'd held this for a few seconds thinking, I guess, that I would afford him an opportunity to insult me one last time. Instead, I just shook my head and stepped over to the front of Fred's cell. He got up from his bunk and came to the bars. I handed him the magazine and pencil and whispered, "If anyone asks, Norma dropped this by."

He nodded and did not question the deception. It may have been he recognized the magazine from Bee's desk and the fact she couldn't play favorites. He said, "Appreciate it."

To me, Fred already looked different. He was sullen like a dog that had got yelled at for digging up some flowers. I said, "How ya fairin'?"

He sighed. "I just need for Monday to hurry up and get here."

I came back, not having any magical cure for the emotional cocktail of boredom, sorrow and uncertainty that he was having to swallow, "Maybe you should just try and catch up on your sleep."

Fred scoffed, "In here?"

And then, as if to validate his point, the hippy, who was now on the other side of Fred began to sing his version of a Righteous Brothers song. He'd no sooner started than the wild man to the left of Billy, shouted, "Shut the hell up."

The hippy paused his singing just long enough to holler back, "Lighten up, dude."

And wild man said, "I'll lighten you up, you silly shit."

The hippy, not the least intimidated, belted out, *You've lost that loving feeling, now it's gone, gone, gone.*

Enraged, wild man shouted, "Screw you."

I took a step to where I could see into the hippy's cell. He was standing, swaying back and forth with his eyes closed and his hands holding an imaginary microphone to his mouth. If wild man would allow it, he'd take himself somewhere else. It was his way of passing the time. I stepped back to the front of Fred's cell. He said, "See what I mean?"

I shrugged. "I know, Fred."

Out of habit, he looked at his wrist where his watch used to be and frowned. "They don't trust a man with nothin' in here."

I said, "It's 2:35."

He sighed. "Four and half hours till Norma comes."

I leaned next to the bars and motioned for him to come whisper close, I said, "The kid next to you is Stroud's son so you may want to watch what you say, maybe not tell him who you are."

"What'd he do?"

"Reckless driving and pot."

"Those damned Californians ain't brought nothing good to this town."

In light of the grief that Stroud had caused me and my in-laws, I couldn't say that I disagreed with Fred but I kept quiet in that regard, I said, "I guess I better go."

I could see in Fred's eyes that much of the animosity he'd had for me at his place this morning was gone. I think it was due to little Freddy Bolander in his blue FFA jacket having surfaced. He said, "Alright, thanks for coming."

<h1 style="text-align:center">CHAPTER ELEVEN</h1>

To be honest, I had truly considered going upstairs and telling Ed Peck about all that I had done since leaving his office this morning. But, the long and the short of it was, my face ached as did two of my teeth that were still seeping just enough blood to discolor my spit and the stab wound in my calf was burning and I didn't have anymore painkillers with me. All of this, and the fact that dealing with Peck wouldn't help any, caused me to radio Millie and tell her that I was done for the day and that I would be home on sick leave.

After changing into some gray sweat pants and a University of Montana Grizzlies tee shirt, I made the ham sandwich that I'd promised myself but opted for ice tea in deference to the warning on my pill bottle about mixing alcohol with it. I was sitting on the patio finishing the last of my sandwich and trying unsuccessfully to not think about today when the phone rang inside the house. I thought seriously of not answering it as the painkiller had made me sleepy and Millie had said she wouldn't call me unless it was a real crisis. But, on the fourth ring I thought, *what if it's Ellen?* This caused me to jump up and immediately smack the knee of my bad leg into the coffee table. I grimaced, "Dammit," and reached to rub it but instantly pulled away as ring number six began. And then, as usual, when a person is in a hurry, the sliding screen door stuck. Ring number eight had just ended and nine was starting when I lifted the phone from its place on the kitchen wall. "Hello."

"Sheriff, this is Ed Peck. Millie told me you'd gone home."

I waited a few seconds for what a normal person might add, somebody who gave a shit, but there was nothing, just Ed's breathing coming back at me. So, I felt free to say, "Yeah, Ed, I feel like crap. In case you hadn't heard, I killed a man yesterday and, in the process, he stabbed me and broke my nose. So, yeah, I'm needin' a little down time. But hey, what can I do for ya?"

"I don't mean to sound indifferent, but why didn't you tell me that you'd arrested Stroud's son. He's mad as hell about it. He thinks you're just trying to get back at him for firing your father-in-law."

"Billy Stroud is guilty as sin."

"Maybe on the traffic charges and simple possession of pot, but Stroud tells me you want to charge his kid with intent to distribute. Is that right?"

"Well, he had more than twice the minimum amount for felony possession and he had a bunch of plastic baggies. So, if you're me, what conclusion would you draw?"

Peck sighed noisily into the phone and then he said, "It's your call, Andy, but I'm hoping you'll go along with making this a simple misdemeanor on the pot."

I smiled and shook my head as I said to myself, *So now it's, Andy.* I said aloud, "No, we both know it'll be your call, Ed. The evidence says otherwise but like I said, it's your call."

"Well now, Andy, I'm not trying to bulldoze you on this but after all, he's just a kid."

The image of Roy reading his draft notice to us flashed in my mind. He wasn't much older than Billy. Wasn't he just a kid? I said, "So, you're going to turn Billy loose?"

"Yes, his father is on his way into town now."

Alright, Ed, if there's nothing else I believe I'm gonna double up on my pain pills and see if I can't get some sleep."

"Good idea, Andy. You do that. Get some sleep."

I hung up the phone wondering if the deal just struck would bode well for Billy on down the line. Not long after this, the second horse pill that I took allowed me to fall asleep on the patio's love seat. It was one of those good slobbery sleeps where you're locked in a dark cave that dream people can't get into. This is where I was when I no longer sensed the soothing warmth of the sun. And then, like a diver slowly coming to the surface, I heard the gentle rattle of ice cubes. As my eyes struggled to open, I heard Ellen say, "Welcome back, sleepyhead."

Still lying on my side, I looked over at her sitting in a lawn chair drinking ice tea. I said, my voice still groggy, "What time is it?

She smiled, "A quarter till nine."

"Nine?"

She laughed. "Yeah, I've been home for a couple of hours. The kids have come and gone."

I sat up. "You should've woke me up. We've could've gone into town and got something to eat."

"No, you were sleeping too sound. You've needed that for quite a while now."

"How was your day? How are your folks doing with the move?"

Ellen sighed. "I don't think it's what my dad thought it was going to be."

"Whaddaya mean?"

"This guy, this Jack Barnes that dad was going to be partners with has changed his mind."

"How so?

"My dad will just be a hired hand. Eight dollars a day and they get to live in this drafty old house that's full of mice. It made my mom cry."

"I'm sorry. They don't deserve this."

Ellen stood and came over to the love seat and sat next to me leaning her head on my chest. She said, her voice a little quivery, "They're too old for this kind of nonsense."

The image of Stroud and the arrogance with which he had fired Phil there on 29 came into my mind as I said, "I know, it's not fair but that's the kind of guy Orville Stroud is."

"You should've seen it, Andy. That house they're moving into is a dump. It's filthy. What little lawn it had died a long time ago. It's mostly dirt, Hon, just bare ground. And you know how much my mom likes her flowers."

I uttered a gentle laugh. "Yeah, she's like her daughter."

"And this house, besides being dirty, it's little. All of their things won't fit in it. My old bedroom furniture and boxes of other stuff are sitting outside in the dirt."

"Barnes doesn't have someplace they can store it?"

"He said they could put it in his shop."

"Oh, I think I've seen it from the road, that metal Quonset building he's got?"

"Yes, it's big and drafty. Some of the floor is cement but most of it is dirt and that's the part where the folks' stuff would have to go, not that it would make much difference, because either way, the mice will have a field day."

"So, how are your folks taking all this?"

"Oh, you know my dad, that old Marine Corps can do attitude. But there were times, I could tell, he was not happy with the situation."

"And your mom?"

"She had tears in her eyes when I left. It was sad, really sad."

And then silence enveloped us, save for the staccato rumble of a motorcycle out on the highway and off in the distance too, a dog barking incessantly. I sensed that Ellen had begun to cry more openly. With my left arm I drew her closer and kissed the top of her head. I stopped short of offering up a solution to her folks' situation as I couldn't think of any that didn't require money. So, we sat there, nestled into one another, listening as the motorcycle got farther and farther away. Its sound was barely audible when the kitchen phone rang. I gave Ellen a final little squeeze. "I'll get it. It's probably for me."

"Oh, I hope not. It's never good at this time of night."

Bella, who had been sleeping near my feet caused me to shuffle my first few steps before I said, "C'mon, Bell dog. I gotta get that phone." She then fell in next to me and followed me inside. I picked up the phone. "Andy, this is Ralph."

I instantly wondered what the owner of the Cedarville store could want with me at this time of night. There were other phones in the little village that were available to anyone. In the few seconds before I responded, I ran through several possible reasons for his call but they were all overshadowed by the likelihood that it had something to do with Stroud. I said, "What can I do for you, Ralph?".

He said, just all at once, "Phil had a heart attack."

His words jolted me to full alert. "What? Are you sure?"

"Ain't none of us doctors, Andy, but that's how Jack Barnes saw it and he was a medic in the Army."

"So, where's Phil?" Behind me. I heard the sliding screen door open.

"Jack and Niko are bringing him to town. They stopped here to call and let the hospital know they were coming so that a doctor would be there. Niko wanted me to call you."

I said, as I looked at the urgency and fear in Ellen's eyes. "Thanks, Ralph. We'll head that way."

Before I got the phone hung up, Ellen asked, "What's happened?"

"They're bringing your dad into the hospital."
"Why?"
"They think he might be having a heart attack."

The emotions from the day that she had only partially corralled, now broke free. She cried and sobbed loudly as she caved into my chest but then, in the next instant, she stepped back and almost shrieked, "We've got to hurry, Andy."

I backed my pickup around and started up Yellow Dog Road towards the highway to town. I turned my red lights on well before the intersection as I had no intention of stopping. It was not quite dark yet. As I neared the stop sign, I could see headlights coming from both directions, they gave no indication of slowing down. I muttered angrily, "C'mon people, give me a break." But on they came. I had no choice but to stop and wait, with my red lights pulsating, while the car from the right blew on by. At the last second, the truck to our left threw on its squeaky brakes and stopped almost directly in front of us. The driver, a man wearing a crumpled white straw cowboy hat, looked at me as if to say he was sorry before grinding the truck into gear and moving on. Ellen looked over for my reaction. I shook my head and then stabbed the gas pedal causing the rear wheels to spray gravel until they grabbed the pavement and we lurched forward. I showed my old pickup no mercy, winding it out in second and third on its way to fourth. We were nearing Brewer's drive-in at the edge of town when Ellen said simply, but louder than necessary, "Andy."

I looked at the speedometer. It read 82, probably faster than Billy Stroud had been going when he locked up the wheels on his GTO and slid into the Buick. I let off the gas and began to brake at the same time as I hit my siren. And so, we went down Main Street with what few cars that were out pulling to the side. I cut my lights and siren just short of the hospital parking lot. Nonetheless, there were several people dressed in green scrubs standing just outside an open door beneath a carport along the side of the hospital. It was where the ambulance unloaded its patients. The scrub people looked our way and then one of them, a slender woman with short dark hair, gestured down the hill but as Ellen and I walked up, they were staring at us. The doctor, a man in his early thirties with wire rim glasses, was the same person that had attended to me after my fight with Joe Garmendia. He stepped towards us and said, like he was surprised, "We thought when we heard the siren you were escorting a patient from the Gros Ventre that we're expecting."

Ellen said, "It's my father. They say he's had a heart attack."

The doctor, whose name was Forney, offered no encouragement other than, "Well, when he gets here, we'll take him right in."

I had no reason to doubt the doctor's abilities as he had done a good job fixing me up but, as I stood there looking at his youthfulness, I couldn't help but wish that he had a few gray hairs around the temples. And that uneasiness lead to wishing that we were at some big hospital in Billings with lots of smart people and the latest gadgetry. But then down the hill, out near the south edge of town, a siren suddenly erupted. Our group, the scrub people and us, all got quiet and listened to its wailing. It was getting louder and louder until there was no doubt as to its destination. And then, when it was close, it abruptly went silent. Its presence foretold only by the rotating strobe of light on the hillside across from the hospital. Seconds later, from the curve just below the lip of the hospital parking lot came the squeal of tires, twice in quick succession. The city police cruiser appeared in the parking lot so quickly that it startled one of the nurses. She jumped back to the doorway of the emergency room. But there was no time to think about whether or not she had over-reacted as the police car pulled to the side and a blue '59 Chevy Impala close behind it screeched to a halt beneath the ambulance canopy. Jack Barnes turned his motor off but it refused to die until it had surged and sputtered a few seconds more. Steam clouded up from beneath the hood, the radiator sounding like a boiling cauldron. Barnes got out of the car, quick and spry for his age, and opened the back door. He helped Niko out. Through the window, I could see that Phil was laying mostly on the seat with his legs cocked to fit in the remaining space. Doctor Forney bent over him with his stethoscope. Almost immediately, he frowned. "Let's get him on the gurney." The nurses, Forney too, were stronger than they looked. They no sooner got Phil on the gurney than the doctor started chest compressions. He shouted, "Let's move, quick." So far, his lack of gray hair didn't seem to be affecting his performance. The wheels of the gurney clattered as they pushed it around the end of the Impala and towards the ER door. Phil's cowboy boots splayed to the sides and his eyes were open but unresponsive. Ellen gasped and pulled her arm from around her mother and ran to the gurney, but the nurses did not slow down. The one with the short dark hair said, "It'd be best if you went to the waiting area." I moved to Ellen's side and put my arm around her shoulders. We could do nothing but watch as her father disappeared through the door into the bright lights of the room beyond it. Suddenly, we were left in the dull light beneath the canopy and the growing darkness beyond it. There was silence of a different kind. The radiator of the Impala continued to boil and its engine, tink, tink, tinking as it cooled. And there were the sobs and sniffles of Ellen and her mother. In the parking lot beyond us, the city police car slowly backed around and started down the hill. I gave him an appreciative wave as I said to the others, "We should go inside."

Barnes said, "I'll move my car, maybe have a smoke and then come in." The bill of his red and white Basin CO-OP hat was inadequate to hide the stress in his face. The continued rebellion of the Chevy's engine suggested it must have been a wild ride coming in. But Jack had plenty of gray hair, possibly proving my theory that with age comes experience and ability or, maybe he was just lucky to have not missed a curve and killed them all.

Niko said, "Thank you, Mr. Barnes."

Barnes looked over at Niko. The light above the door reflected in his watery eyes as he said, "I'm sorry." His words sounded inadequate and heavy with guilt.

Niko nodded but said nothing before turning away with Ellen's arm around her. They started toward the hospital's front door.

I looked at Jack and for a brief moment considered telling him that it was ok if he wanted to go home, that it was getting late and he had a long way to go and his wife would be concerned, but I said, "I guess we'll see you inside."

He nodded, "Yeah, I'll be along in a minute."

I hurried to catch up with Ellen and Niko. I'd just reached them when I heard from behind me the Chevy fire up and begin to move. But then things didn't sound right for what Jack said he was going to do. I looked around as did Ellen and her mother. The taillights of the Chevy were just dropping out of sight down the hill from the parking lot.

Niko said, "I think it was eating him up."

"What was?" said Ellen.

"Phil and Barnes were arguing just before your father collapsed."

"What were they arguing about?"

"All of it, just all of it. To go from the good life we had to, well, you saw it."

Ellen nodded. "I know, Mom, but things will get better, you'll see."

But they did not. We were in the waiting area not quite 20 minutes when the doctor came out. The second he opened the ER door his face took away even a sliver of hope. He stopped five or six feet from us and did not hesitate, he said, "I'm sorry. We just couldn't revive him."

Ellen and her mother caved into one another and began to cry. I looked at Forney and wondered if we had been in Billings if things would have turned out differently. But truth be told, I could see that Phil was dead when they took him out of the car. So, who was to blame? Barnes and the stress he caused? Or maybe where it all started, Orville Stroud? But in the back of my mind I was having trouble suppressing the naysayer in me. *If you had a job that didn't require you to be in the middle of all the bad things that happen in this county, you wouldn't have had that chance meeting with Phil that got him fired. He and Niko would be coming for Sunday dinner to see Roy off to the service.* I sighed, knowing all too well there would be countless nights to assign blame. I said to Forney, "I appreciate your trying."

Before we left, they allowed us to go back and see Phil. I guess it was like saying, *we're not so rude that just because you're dead, we won't come say goodnight.* He was covered with a white sheet from the neck down. Niko kissed him on the lips and then hugged him through the sheet while Ellen looked on, quietly crying and waiting her turn. As they moved back, I touched Phil on the shoulder half expecting him to open his eyes and say to me in that jovial voice of his, *Its' been a helluva night. I could use a cold one, how 'bout you?* I wondered, as I had so many times over the years when it came to dead people, if Phil's ledger had enough check marks in the plus column to warrant his spirit being there with us, or if it had gone elsewhere. Although he was not a church goer, I was confident that the system would have to be flawed if he wasn't there. I said in a normal voice, "We'll see ya later, Phil."

Just outside the door to the ER, Forney stopped me. He said, "We can call O'Leary's for you and have them come for the body, if you want"

Although it was Niko's call to make, I said, "I believe we'll go with Reinecker's." For some reason, I just couldn't see having Raymond tending to something as personal as this would be to us.

We idled down the hill from the hospital. Ellen was sitting next to me allowing her mother the air from the open window. We were still in the nicer part of town. There was just enough light to generate comments about this person's flowers or the color of a house had the circumstances been different but instead, we rode along with nobody talking. Down low in the background, the radio was playing. I guess it was just force of habit or the stillness, but I turned it up. Within seconds, I regretted it. A Sonny James song was playing. *You're the only world I know, you're the one I can't let go, you're my laughter and my tears and I love you all my years, you're-* Niko began to cry aloud. I instantly felt bad, but even worse when Ellen shot me a dirty look and turned the radio off.

I whispered, "I'm sorry."

It was a little before ten when we got home. Roy and Emma were still out with their friends, which was fine with me as I was not looking forward to telling them that their grandpa was dead. And too, it made it a little easier to convince Niko to take Emma's room tonight. She had a bad headache due, I suppose, to all that had happened and only politely resisted before taking one of my pain pills and going to bed. Ellen sat with her and they talked and cried until almost eleven. And then we sat on the couch and watched tv and waited for the kids to come home.

CHAPTER TWELVE

On Monday morning, Ellen and her mother made bacon and eggs and sourdough hotcakes. Although food seemed secondary, having to prepare it pushed aside the sorrow in their minds if only for a little while. It had been a long weekend, spent mostly making Phil's funeral arrangements. As it looked, Tuesday, the same day that Roy was to report for his physical, was the earliest that it could take place.

We were all there, except Phil, seated at the kitchen table. Ellen had been pestering the food on her plate for almost ten minutes and still hadn't made much of a dent in it. From the chair next to her mother she looked straight across the table at me and said, out of the blue, "I still think it wouldn't hurt to call the draft board and see if Roy can't put off when he has to report. Surely, they would give him time to grieve, don't you think?"

I laid my fork down so as to not appear indifferent, I said, "A person would think so, but you got to remember this is the government you're dealing with."

She said, as if I was deaf or didn't understand, "but his grandpa has just died."

I said, hoping to not open another can of sorrow for Niko, "23 years ago the government locked your grandparents up in an internment camp. You think they're more compassionate now?"

Roy cut in, "Just let it go, the both of you. I've got a ride down to Livingston tomorrow. It's all set up."

I said, "I was figuring on taking you. The funeral isn't until one o'clock."

Roy shook his head. "It's alright dad. This way only one of us has to get up in the middle of the night so I can be down there by 6:30 a.m." He paused and then looked at Niko. "Grandma, I hope you don't think that I don't want to be at Grandpa's funeral because I do. It's just, well, I'm afraid of this. I'm not as strong as grandpa was. Not going in the morning and having more time to think about all of this wouldn't be good for me. I guess maybe I'm being selfish."

Niko said, her voice filled with concern, "No, Roy, if your grandpa was here, he'd tell you to do just what you are."

"Thanks, Grandma, I appreciate your understanding."

I quickly raised my cup to take a drink of coffee so as to hide the disappointment in my face. No one, I thought, was the wiser until I saw Ellen looking at me, she knew.

At 4:30 on Tuesday morning, we all came together again at the kitchen table for toast and coffee and to say goodbye to Roy. We skirted around the white elephant in the room and talked of mundane things like the weather and Gros Ventre County High's upcoming football schedule and the rest of fire season. At times, there was even laughter and it was almost like Phil wasn't dead and Roy wasn't going off to possibly follow after his grandpa. But then headlights shone through the kitchen window and the rigid finality of some things in life came back to us all. It may have prompted Ellen to say, "Now you be sure and talk to the Air Force recruiter. Just think how nice it would be if you could get stationed right up here at Great Falls. Now, you remember to do that, Roy."

"Ok, Mom, I will."

And then there was a round of hugs and kisses and *I love you*'s as we all trailed out through the garage to the car waiting in the driveway. We clustered in the headlights and waved and shouted like it was his first day of school. The car, a brown '64 Chevy station wagon, was crowded with people. I was hoping that Roy would roll down his window and wave, but he didn't. We continued to watch until the taillights reached the highway and turned south. I pulled Ellen closer to me. In the darkness, I could feel her crying.

With the exception of Emma, who went back to bed, we all topped off our coffees and went out on the patio. Ellen and her mom sat on the love seat while I took a chair across from them with Bella laying at my feet. No one bothered to turn the light on so we sat there in the near darkness. I suspect it was the way everyone wanted it as there didn't seem to be anything good to talk about. Just beyond the house, in the trees by the river, a Great Horned owl hooted. Bella raised her head and looked in that direction and gave a low growl. But it was as if she was in the presence of statues, as nobody said a word. Finally, Niko stated what was common knowledge to all of us, "So, we have to be at the funeral home by eleven?"

I said, "Yes, Reinecker wants to be out to Cedarville by 11:30 for the viewing."

In the poor light I could not read her eyes but I could see Niko shake her head, she said, "I don't know if Phil would want people looking at him."

Ellen said, "You don't have to, Mom, but it's what was in the paper."

"Oh, I know. People will think we're hiding something if we don't open the casket. You know how they are."

"It should be a real nice service. You saw yesterday how many flowers have already been delivered to the funeral home."

Niko nodded, "Yes, Phil had lots of friends in the valley. He was never one to tell a person no if they needed help. Not everyone out there can make that claim." She paused, as if she was uncertain to say it but then she did, "For sure, Orville Stroud can't. I checked the list. He didn't even bother to send flowers."

Ellen said, "Why should that surprise you?"

"That man isn't real savvy about the land and livestock. Your father helped him a lot."

Pangs of guilt welled up within me. *If only I hadn't run into Phil that day. We wouldn't be sitting here having this conversation.*

Niko looked my way. "The men from the Legion are all set?"

I said, "Yes, they'll be there. It will be a military service, everything they do, the rifle volleys, taps and folding the flag, it-"

"I know, Andy. Remember, I've done this before at the Cedarville cemetery, no less."

My mind flashed back 23 years ago to where Ellen's brother, Melvin, lay dead beneath a big ponderosa pine with a pistol still clutched in his hand. I was a brand-new deputy at the time, but all these years later I can still visualize it like it just happened.

Niko said, "I'm sorry, I didn't mean to be short."

"It's ok."

She sighed, "Today just needs to be over." And then she may have realized that after today, Phil, in a physical sense, would be gone forever and she began to cry.

CHAPTER THIRTEEN

The little community church on the edge of Cedarville over-flowed with people in attendance to Phil's funeral. As expected, Orville Stroud was not among them, nor were any of his other hands as he wouldn't give them time off to come. But it was done now and Phil lay next to his son, Melvin. The grass surrounding their graves was brown due to not being watered on a regular basis. I promised Niko that I would look into it.

We had expected to hear from Roy on Tuesday afternoon or evening to let us know how his physical turned out and what the Air Force had said, but he didn't call. So, here it was Wednesday morning. I was still off work trying to line up a moving company to just go get all of Niko's belongings and bring them to a storage facility here in town. I'd also checked in with Millie and learned that Fred's bail had been set at $25,000 and he was still in jail pending Norma being able to come up with the ten percent required by a Great Falls bail bondsman. There was little doubt in my mind that my name was probably mud at the Bolander house. The money to pay a bail bondsman had probably gone to pay for Teddy's funeral.

Ellen and her mother were in Roy's room boxing up his things so Niko would have space for her things. Today was the fifth day that Phil had been dead. Niko had told Ellen, *it's the nights that are hardest to take.* I had no problem with Niko coming to live with us as Ellen was hurting too.

I was sitting at the kitchen table, sipping a cup of luke-warm coffee, when the phone rang. I hollered down the hall towards Roy's bedroom, "I'll get it." I lifted the receiver, "Hello."

"Hi Dad, I've just got a minute."

"How'd things go? We've been kinda worried since we didn't hear from you yesterday."

"Well, according to the military, I'm fit as a fiddle."

"And the Air Force, how'd it go with them?"

I was met with silence, like he hadn't heard me. In the background I could hear a loudspeaker announce, *Flight 2219 to Denver now boarding.* I said again, "And the Air Force?"

"I joined the Marines, Dad."

I was taken aback, but not entirely surprised. Ellen would not be happy, but there was no point in picking his decision apart. I said, "So, where are you going?"

He said, already sounding kind of military like, "Marine Corps Recruit Depot at San Diego." And then he added, "Grandpa Phil would be proud, don't you think?"

Phil had been in France during World War I. He had medals on account of he had been shot and gassed and no doubt killed people, but he seldom ever talked about it. I had to wonder how he would have advised Roy? I said, "How long are you in for?"

"Two years, but they say if you go to Vietnam, when you come back you'll be so short that they'll discharge you."

The words, *when you come back*, echoed in my mind but I didn't point them out, I said, "Let me holler at your mother, her and Grandma will want to talk to you."

"Tom's here, Dad. I've got to go."

"Whose Tom?"

"Tom Piva, the guy that I rode up here with. We're going in on the buddy plan."

"Buddy plan? Where'd this come from?" Before Roy could answer, I felt Ellen's hand on my shoulder. I said, "Here's your mother."

"Roy, where are you?"

"I'm sorry, Mom. I've got to go. Dad can fill you in. Love you."

Ellen said, frantically, "I love you, call when you get there." But even I could hear the dial tone. I could see the hurt in her eyes. She said, "Why didn't you come get me?"

"I'd barely started talking to him."

"What did he say?"

I shook my head. "He joined the Marines."

"What? How could he do that after all that we'd talked about the Air Force?"

"I don't know. He's fixed on the notion that he can get out in less than two years if he goes to Vietnam."

Ellen's eyes were still red from all of the crying she had done yesterday but, at the mention of Vietnam, they teared up again. Last night we'd both watched Walter Cronkite tell about some big battle the Marines were involved in. There were hundreds of Viet Cong killed but they showed dead Marines too. She'd said, like it was a panacea to not die, *I'm so glad Roy will be going into the Air Force. It will be nice to have him close to home.* At the time I kept quiet as we'd had enough grief for one day, but I couldn't help but be suspicious of the fact Roy hadn't even bothered to call the Air Force recruiter during the time from when he got his draft notice till now. All of a sudden, she collected herself and looked at me as if to gauge my response, "Did you know he was going to do this? Because if you did, it's not right that the two of you would keep it from me."

Beyond Ellen, her mother said in a gentle voice, "It's just how boys are."

"Exactly, Mom, he's a boy."

I said, "He hasn't been a boy since he started fighting fire."

Ellen laughed sarcastically. "Not that he needs it, but the state of Montana still says he isn't old enough to drink." She scoffed, "How does that work, you're mature enough to kill somebody but not buy a beer?"

Ellen stormed from the kitchen out to the patio. Neither her mother or I had any good answers. Niko said, "I'll go talk to her."

I nodded just as the phone on the wall began to ring. It was the movers. They were coming down from Great Falls but didn't know where to go. We agreed to meet at ten tomorrow morning in Cedarville so I could lead them out to the Barnes' place. For Niko, it would be going away from a life that had brought her security and happiness to one of longing for the past.

The next day, the three of us, Niko, Ellen and I, drove out to Cedarville and then on to Jack's with the Mayflower boys in tow. I'd told Jack at the funeral of my intentions to hire a moving company. So, whether it was by design or coincidence, he and his wife got in their car not long after we got there and drove off. In his defense, I suppose a person can only say they're sorry so many times. And on the flip side of that, how many times was Niko expected to say, *no, Jack, things just happen, when in truth she wanted to say, if you'd been honest about everything we'd never have come here and stressed Phil's heart and he'd be alive because we'd be living in town.* But Jack left the premises and by four o'clock when we closed the door on the moving van they still hadn't come back. Although there was no need to follow one another, as I had given the Mayflower boys the address of the storage facility, we headed out putting up two tandem rooster tails of dust. The movers were getting the worst of this arrangement, but it couldn't be helped unless one of us peeled off and took a different and longer route. There was a somber mood in the car knowing that the Lujack family, or what was left of it, was leaving the valley after all these years. However, that air of melancholy abruptly went away as just turning off of CR29 and coming towards us was a blue Chevy pickup that looked a lot like Orville Stroud's. What didn't jive was the fact the pickup had fish-tailed wildly when it came off the pavement onto the gravel and it was now accelerating real fast. I said, "Look at this fool. Coming at us like hell wouldn't have it on this narrow road and here I am, in a civilian car and clothes." I slowed some and pulled over as far as I dared and then we passed. I erupted, "Why that little shit, he's not supposed to be driving."

"Who was that?" asked Ellen.

"Billy Stroud. He should still be in jail, but that's another matter. What I do know for sure is he doesn't have a driver's license."

Ellen read into my anger and frustration, she said, "You could follow him home, I guess and-"

I laughed. "And what? No, today is Billy's lucky day." I laughed some more and then added, "Who says cops aren't nice guys." Until a minute ago I was taking some solace in the fact that we were helping Niko start a new life without her best friend but thanks to Billy Stroud, that now seemed a little tainted.

CHAPTER FOURTEEN

Phil had been dead eleven days now. The future for Niko, and us too, was beginning to take shape. At age 63 she wasn't quite old enough to collect social security and even if she could, what was she to do, sit at our house and watch soap operas all day? If she'd been better off financially she could possibly have bought herself a little house and gardened and got a part-time job somewhere. But the reality of it all was she was nearly broke, that was why at age 65 Phil was starting over at Jack Barnes' place.

After supper we migrated to the patio as had become our routine. I sat in the chair that faced to the west. Ellen and her mother, as usual, occupied the love seat. Thunder rumbled overhead causing Bella to get up and go inside.

Niko said, "Why is it dogs hate thunder so much?"

"And fireworks and gun shots," added Ellen as she looked at me like I would tell them why.

I looked up at the dark cumulus clouds and laughed. "What was it Roy called these clouds, cumulus overtimus?"

It took a few seconds for it to sink in, but then Ellen and Niko laughed. Ellen said, "Yeah, I imagine the fire crew will be busy tonight."

Niko added, "Out in the Gros Ventre these thunder storms always had the forest service hopping."

I said, "Yeah, Roy would've been in hog heaven tonight."

Ellen took a sip of her Coke and then looked at me, she said, "Do you suppose the Marines will ever let Roy write us an actual letter. That stupid post card we got a couple of days ago said next to nothing."

"We know he's there and he's safe."

Ellen frowned like I was siding with the Marines. She moved on. "I noticed on my way home from work that your campaign sign just this side of the drive-in was knocked down."

"Yeah, I saw it too."

"Did you stop and put it up?"

"No, I did that a couple of days ago. Seems somebody wants me to know that I'm being dropped from their Christmas card list."

Niko gave me a confused look. "They what?"

"They're not happy with me."

"But your job, aren't you concerned?"

I shrugged. "I don't know. There's some days when I think how nice it would be to not have to clean up car wrecks or fight with drunks or hot-headed sheep herders. And not get calls at all hours of the night." I laughed, "Maybe just work for Jake's Feed and Seed."

"Surely, you don't mean that. You don't want to end up like me."

"Like you?"

"I have no savings, Andy. We had it all in that new packing plant that went bankrupt up at Great Falls."

"I'm sorry."

"That's what crooked people will do for you. Took our life savings. So, don't you take your job lightly. You'll need the pension that goes with it."

I wanted to say, *but at what price*? Instead, I nodded, "That's probably good advice." I knew, however, that I wasn't going to put up that campaign sign again.

Ellen jumped in before her mother could continue, "Would either of you like something to drink?"

I said, "A Budweiser sounds good, with a glass."

Ellen smiled. "There better be a good tip in this for me."

Niko stood up. "I'll take an ice tea, but I can get it."

Ellen said, "I'll get it, Mom," but by then Niko was through the sliding door and into the living room.

I looked to the timber covered mountains west of town. Periodically, lightning razored down from the black clouds overhead. To myself, I counted the seconds until I heard the thunder that accompanied these stabs of brilliance. I made a note to myself to write Roy and tell him about this storm.

In the morning, the skies over the house were clear and the ground was damp to the point it had settled the dust. Ellen had been called in to work a little after 4:00 A.M. on account of the forest service was setting up a fire camp on Pistol Creek and they needed someone with purchase authority. I had figured on making my own breakfast, but Niko had it ready for me when I got out of the shower. I said, "You didn't have to do this."

She said, "A person can only stare at the ceiling so long."

CHAPTER FIFTEEN

Phil had been dead 33 days and Teddy Bolander and Stroud's sheep herders slightly longer. Outwardly, it appeared that Niko's emotional wound was healing, not completely by any means, but scabbed over to the point that she had started working as a part-time checker at the IGA. She insisted on helping out with food, to which we agreed. However, on the other hand, I had not seen Fred Bolander since I booked him into jail. In response to my inquiry, Ed Peck had told me that Fred had posted bail and hired old Herb Boyer to represent him. How this arrangement was working out I did not know, until the morning of September 18th. I had just parked my pickup in front of the courthouse and was coming up the sidewalk when out of the big front doors came Herb, Norma and Owen. Norma was crying. I was still a good 15 or 20 feet away when Owen glared at me and shouted, "Well, you sonovabitch, you ought to be happy now."

Herb immediately held his arm out in front of Owen like it was a stop sign on a school bus. "You're not helping matters, Owen."

Norma sobbed, "Just let it go. You can't help your dad now."

"No, this asshole needs to know the pain he's caused this family. Him and that fat little faggot DA."

Herb tried again, "Shut up, Owen. You can't be doing this without there being consequences."

I knew that Fred had struck a deal with Peck to plead guilty if he would reduce the charge to aggravated assault. Today was his day to go before the judge. I said to Owen, "I'm tolerant to a point and then you need to rein in your name calling. And I gotta tell ya, you're getting real close to that point."

Owen snorted like I was deserving of no respect at all. He sneered at me, "You know how many calves we had to sell, under-weight calves to boot. Huh? 57, that's how many. But you wouldn't know anything about that with your cushy government job. Why, we coulda put another 120 pounds on those calves but no, we had to sell 'em early so we could pay this fella and the bail bondsman and the funeral home. We need to send that damned Stroud the bill for all of this. He's the one that started it all. He's the one that should be going to Deerlodge, not my dad."

I said, trying to sound sympathetic, "What did the judge give your father?"

"Five years. Can you believe that shit? That fat little toad of a DA was talking six months to a year, right here, not in Deerlodge."

I looked around. We had drawn a crowd. Owen insulting me the way he was would make good bar room talk if it got around, and I had little doubt that it wouldn't. I said, more to Norma than Owen, "I'm sorry to hear this."

At first, her eyes suggested that my words were important to her, but then she looked away and said to Owen, "Let's just go home."

Owen scowled at me, he said, "You know, what goes around comes around."

"So, what's that supposed to mean?"

He laughed derisively, "You're the big shot law man, you figure it out."

Herb stepped in front of Owen. He said, "Your mother doesn't need this, go home."

Owen snorted and then said, "Well, I guess maybe we should while we still got a home to go to." And then they walked on towards their car, the painful awkward silence being broken only by Norma quietly crying and the clicking of her high heels on the sidewalk. In that same moment, I could feel the stares of a half dozen people, standing there like they'd just been treated to a mini soap opera. I briefly scanned their faces and then walked away. Lost votes? I didn't care.

I climbed the steps to the second floor and Ed Peck's office. The hallway was empty. At the far end of it the doors to the court room, where Fred had just been sentenced, stood open. For now, the stately room was abandoned by everyone who'd had a part in denying Fred his freedom for the next five years. But tomorrow or next week or next month, someone else would likely get their dose of misery in there. I'd sometimes thought, in one of my more philosophical moments, if walls were like people, how could these absorb so much sadness and anger? My appointment with Peck, and the board who had reviewed my shooting of Joe Garmendia, was scheduled for three o'clock. At five minutes till, I opened the door to Peck's office.

Angie pushed back from her typewriter and reached for the phone. Midway in this, she said, "Hi Andy, I'll tell them you're here."

Had the door to Peck's inner office been open I would have just knocked on the door frame and announced myself, but it was not. It may have been my paranoia or dislike of Peck, but this whole thing of having to be announced seemed pretentious to me.

Angie clunked her black phone down on the receiver. "You can go in now."

I glanced over at her, "Thanks," and opened the door. I did not remove my white straw cowboy hat as, after all, this was Montana. The moment I stepped inside the three of them, Peck, the sheriff from the next county over, and a sergeant from the highway patrol, all got quiet.

Peck said, "Have a chair, Andy." He then gestured to the others, "I believe you know these fellas."

I nodded towards the two men who were sitting on the left side of a dark cherry wood table that sat in front of Peck's desk, which was made of the same material. I knew the men but not real well. I said, "How you boys fairin' today?"

They came back with kind of a collective mumble, "Doing good."

Peck, who was sitting at the end of the table nearest his desk, motioned for me to sit down across from the other men. He then looked over at the state trooper and said, "Carl, why don't you start us off?"

The trooper in his neatly pressed uniform and flat top haircut appeared to be all business. He said, "Well Sheriff, we've looked pretty hard at the circumstance that caused you to have to use your sidearm to defend yourself and we've concluded that it was justifiable." He then paused and briefly glanced over at his partner before easing into what came next, he said, "But, what does concern us is how Mr. Garmendia got the drop on you? It kind of speaks to the necessity of all this."

My heart gathered speed as the adrenaline began to flow within me, I said, "Well, he bum- rushed me from behind. Knocked me down. There wasn't much I could do."

At this point, the sheriff, whose name was Wiley Holbert, jumped in, he said, "We're wondering how it was that you turned your back on him?"

Phil's warning flashed in my mind but I said, "I guess I didn't think he was a risk to jump me."

"What we're hearing at the Antler Bar in Cedarville is this Garmendia fella was somebody you didn't want to mess with, especially if he's been drinking."

"Well, as far as I know he was stone cold sober when he and I tangled."

Wiley nodded. "Yeah, the autopsy bears that out but the ditch rider out on the Gros Ventre says he and Garmendia nearly had fisticuffs over how much water Stroud was not getting. You ever hear anything about that?"

I said to myself, *this must have been why Phil warned me about him.* I truthfully said aloud, "I've never heard anything about a water dispute or trouble at the Antler."

Wiley paused and looked at me with a renewed intensity and said, "I guess what we're getting at here, Andy, is your judgement. We feel like you should have known better than to turn your back on this guy but even more than that, with this guy's reputation, we question why you didn't take someone else with you."

For a moment I was speechless, wrapped up in my own pity party, I guess. Just a short time ago I had been verbally assaulted by Owen Bolander and now here I was having my intelligence questioned by my peers. It was a little overwhelming. All three of them just sat there waiting, I imagined, to jump on whatever I said next. Finally, I said, "Do you have any other criticisms of me?"

Carl appeared embarrassed, Wiley less so, but Peck said, "You will be exonerated in the killing of Joe Garmendia, but these issues of judgement will be noted in the final report and made a part of your personnel file."

Anger instantly consumed me. I was sure that it was visible in my face, in fact I hoped it was. I said, "Have you got anything else for me?"

Peck slid a copy of the report across the table to me. "If you agree, sign on the line by your name."

I scoffed, "I guess I don't have much choice."

"You can protest it but you never know how they may view it."

I gave Peck a, *go to hell look*, and said, "Yeah, you never know." I signed the paper and left it lay where it was. I stood up, "That it?"

Peck nodded, "Yes, that's it."

I ignored Carl and Wiley and walked out. In the outer office I purposely said, in a loud cheerful voice, "See ya, Angie. Have a good evening."

My anger caused me to walk faster than I normally did. Inwardly, I knew the board was right. I'd been complacent, I should have heeded Phil's warning and called Cheevers to go with me. At a minimum, I should never have turned my back on Joe. Twenty-three years on the job, what was I thinking?

I did not share with Millie all that the board had said, just the part about me being justified in shooting Garmendia. She, of course, now felt free to tell me that she had to set straight a couple of ladies in her book club that thought, *it was just terrible that I'd killed that poor sheep herder*. I thanked her for sticking up for me but, at the same time, wondered how many other similar conversations were taking place around the county where nobody took my side.

Our mailbox was the bright yellow one with red and blue daisy looking flowers. It had been Emma's idea to paint the drab metal box with its little red flag. She was right when she said, *you'll never confuse ours with any of the other umpteen boxes there*. I slowed at the bank of boxes next to the highway, when in the distance, I saw Ellen driving down Yellow Dog road towards our house. In the past, before Roy had gone into the Marines, there would be no guarantee that she had stopped for the mail but now I knew better. So far, we had gotten the post card and three letters from Roy. To say that we looked forward to hearing from him would be well beyond an understatement. It was kind of like our lives back here, even with all of the freedoms, had become dull in comparison to what Roy was doing. At least, this is the way I felt.

I'd no sooner stepped into the kitchen when I saw the mail on the table. There were two piles; one with bills, junk and the October issue of Outdoor Life magazine, and off to the side, by itself, a letter from Roy.

"Hi, Honey."

I looked up. Ellen was coming down the hall. She'd changed into faded jeans and a Disneyland tee shirt. I said, "How's my favorite Mouseketeer?"

She smiled and looked up at me for a kiss. As she pulled away, she said, her voice carefree, "We got a letter from Roy."

"I saw that."

"You want to get something to drink and read it out on the patio?"

"Sounds good. How 'bout I feed Bella while you get the drinks?"

"Ok, ice tea, beer or me?"

I laughed. "Don't tempt me."

Ellen smiled. "So, I take it you want a Bud?"

"Yeah, that sounds good."

"With a glass?"

I looked over to where Ellen was just getting in the fridge. She was looking back at me with a mischievous grin. I stepped closer and slapped her on the butt as I went by. I said, playfully, "yeah, with a glass."

We then both broke into laughter. It was always good to be home with her.

For September, it was exceptionally warm. We placed our drinks on the coffee table and sat down next to one another on the love seat. Ellen held the letter out to me, "You wanna open it?"

"You go ahead."

She did not hesitate to tear open the envelope. She began to read:

Dear Mom, Dad, Grandma, Emma and Bella,

I laughed, "You'd think he'd just say, dear family."

Ellen smiled, "I guess he doesn't want anyone to feel left out."

"I guess not."

Ellen went on:

I hope all is well with you guys. Judging from your last letter, it sounds like it has been a nice fall there and I have been missing out on lots of fires. Oh well, in less than two years I'll be back at it and going to school at MSU on the GI Bill. How cool will that be?

Next week, we get to go to the rifle range. It will be a welcome break from the endless marching and PT that we do every day. I have to say, though, that I do like the obstacle course. Some of the guys are so out of shape it is tough for them, but I guess if they do enough PT they'll be able to handle it someday. However, for three of our guys that day didn't come soon enough. They just pretty much gave up -totally. The next thing we knew was them, and all of their stuff, was gone. I have to admit, when I first got here, it was tempting to do what these guys did but I'm so glad that I stuck it out. You just have to learn that this is kind of a game and the quicker you learn the rules the better off you'll be. I don't know how these poor slobs that washed out will ever be able to show their faces back home. I'm glad I had my time fighting fire. It prepared me for the long days here. It seems like we never get to sleep or at least not very much.

Grandma, how are you doing. Good, I hope. I think I know now why Grandpa was so proud to be a Marine, I never told him but I was proud to have him as my Grandpa.

At this point, Ellen paused reading as she had begun to cry. I put my arm around her and squeezed her shoulder. "You want me to finish it?"

She nodded as she wiped her eyes.

I continued:

Grandpa was the old Corps. He could definitely teach some of these kids a thing or two about just sucking it up and driving on.

How's Fremont doing in football? I'll miss not being able to go to the games. I'm going to miss too not hunting deer this fall. It'll probably be the same way next fall too but the fall of '67 the deer had better watch out. Dad, you had better count on us going hunting then. Well, I better go. They just dimmed the lights. That means they'll be turned off in five minutes. Give Bella a pet from me.

Love to all,
Roy

P.S. Mom please don't send anymore cookies. We can't have food in the barracks.

I laid the letter on the coffee table. "Sounds like he's doing alright."

Ellen nodded as she continued to dab at her eyes. She said, "For now he is."

CHAPTER SIXTEEN

It was on the fifth of December that I saw Owen Bolander yet again. I was approaching the Sinclair station on the north edge of town when he pulled out in his father's pickup and headed up the valley. Over the past several months I had seen him probably a half dozen times. It wasn't that I was keeping tabs on him but, it was my impression, way back when we had our differences, that he was just temporarily home on leave. Dick McFarland, a friend of Roy's that I knew fairly well, appeared to have spotted my truck and was standing by the gas pumps in anticipation of waving as I drove by. I had not planned on getting gas but my curiosity had gotten the better of me, so I turned into the station and stopped at the pump next to Dick. It was cold. His breath pulsated in the air before him. As I opened my door he started removing my gas cap and said, "Whaddaya know, Andy? I'd say she's colder 'n a witch's tit, don't you think?"

I laughed politely. "I can't say that I've ever hung out with any witches, so I'll just take your word for it."

He looked back at me and grinned before inserting the nozzle into my tank and starting the gas. A big round thermometer with a plexiglass face hung on the wall next to the door of the station. Dick nodded towards it. "It was five below when I came to work this morning."

It being close to noon, I said, "Well, there ain't no heat wave on now."

"It could be worse. The guy that was just in here said it was 17 below at his house last night."

I said innocently, "Wasn't that Owen Bolander?"

"Yeah, he lives way hell and gone up – " Dick abruptly paused and then said, "well, I guess you know where he lives."

I nodded. "I thought he was in the Army?"

"Well, I guess he still is."

"Whaddaya mean?"

Dick seemed hesitant to say it but then he just put it out there. "I guess with all that's happened to his family and his mother being left alone to run the place, the Army agreed to let Owen out early if he'd go into the national guard. That's why he was in here, gassin' up so he can drive to Great Falls in the morning. He said he's got to play Army this weekend."

"Well, good for his mother. I'm sure this will make her life easier."

Dick snorted and tossed his head. "I don't know."

"Whaddaya mean, you don't know?"

After looking around, not so much to see if anybody might be within hearing distance but rather if there was anyone that might be watching him talk to me, he said, "I ain't so sure him and the national guard might not have a train wreck."

"Why's that?"

"A couple of weeks ago he came in smelling like pot. I guess he thought I was looking at him funny so he just out of the blue asks me if I wanted to get high? I told him no but he badgered me for close to ten minutes trying to get me to smoke a joint with him. He finally left but I wondered at the time how much help he was going to be to his mother."

I sighed and shook my head. "I'm sorry to hear that."

Dick moved on, like he hadn't just squealed on Owen. He said, as he removed the nozzle, "Didn't take much today.

Buck twenty-seven, you want me to put it on the county's tab?"

"Yeah, they got more money than I do."

"Your oil ok?"

"It's ok, Dick. Go inside and get warm."

"Thanks, Andy."

As I drove off, I wished that Dick hadn't told me about Owen and the pot. It would be the final nail in the Bolander family coffin if I was to arrest him for possession of marijuana.

The remainder of the day was miserably cold. The sun, for what little good it had done, was already behind the mountains as I turned onto Yellow Dog Road. Ellen and Emma were home. Niko, being the low person on the totem pole of seniority at the IGA, was working till eight o'clock. Bella was first to greet me as I stepped into the utility room. I reached down and ruffled her ears and then started for the kitchen. Ellen was standing at the stove tending a pan of sizzling pork chops on one burner and sliced spuds in the skillet next to it. She said, "Hi Hon," and then turned to give me a kiss.

I gave her a peck on the lips and then said, trying not to grin, "You know, if somebody could bottle the smell of fried pork chops, I bet they could make money selling it."

Ellen looked at me and rolled her eyes. "I don't think I'll invest in that outfit."

"No seriously, fried pork chops and fresh brewed coffee, nothing better."

She nodded towards the coffee pot on the counter. "Well, have at it."

"Ok, I'll make a pot then. Your mom will probably want some when she gets home. It's that kind of weather." I'd just reached for the white crock cannister next to the coffee pot when the phone rang. Instinctively, I looked at the clock on the wall it read, 5:40. In the next instant I heard Emma's bedroom door open followed by, "I'll get it," and running steps in the hall.

"Hello, yes, just a second."

I'd already started walking towards Emma. She held the phone down at her side and whispered, "It's Ed Peck."

I tried not to frown. "Thanks." I took a deep breath and exhaled before putting the phone to my mouth. I said, not necessarily trying to be friendly but just civil, "You're working late for a Friday night."

I could hear him sigh into the phone and then he said, "I just got a call from Deerlodge. Fred Bolander is dead."

"What? How did that happen?"

"A fight,"

"Over what?"

"They don't know for sure. I guess there's some speculation that Bolander had gotten some kind of tough guy reputation since he was in there for beating a man to death."

"Are you kidding me?"

Peck ignored my outburst. He said, knowing full well that I wouldn't, "Can you send your deputy to inform Bolander's wife of what's happened?"

I did not hesitate, "No, I'll go."

"Why be a martyr, Andy? Send your deputy."

"That wouldn't be right, not this time."

"Suit yourself. Tell them the body will be available for pickup on Monday."

I shook my head. Maybe it was just me but he seemed indifferent to it all. I said, "Alright, I'll go tonight and tell Norma. She'll be devastated."

"Ok, I'll let you know if I hear anything else from the prison. Goodbye, Andy."

I hung up the phone. By the looks on their faces it was obvious that Ellen and Emma had deduced what had happened. I said anyway, "Fred's been killed in a prison fight. I've got to run out to the Bolander place."

Ellen stepped close to me. She said emphatically as she placed her hand on my chest and looked up at me, "You be careful. You know how hot-headed Owen can be."

I leaned down and kissed her and then said with a grin, "I will, you guys save me a pork chop." And then I gave her a hug and left.

It wasn't totally dark as I drove out Yellow Dog Road, but it was dark enough that I turned on my headlights. By the time I reached the turnoff for the Elk Creek Road, I could see stars overhead and a half moon behind me. Barely a month ago, enough of the voters had saw fit to keep me on their Christmas card list for another four years. It gave my ego a boost but I still wondered at times how my life might have changed had I been forced to find another job, maybe with Jake's Feed and Seed or some such. Why right now, I could be home eating a pork chop and some fried spuds in a warm house. And then I came back to reality as two deer ran across the road in front of me. I braked until they had jumped the barbed wire fence to my right and escaped out into the pasture beyond it. I accelerated slowly knowing that in a few minutes I would be standing before Norma and destroying the rest of her life. All too soon I went across the wooden bridge over Elk Creek, thumping loudly, its one loose plank. As I idled up the dirt road to the house, I rehearsed in my mind how best to tell her that Fred was dead. But there was no good way. I'd no sooner parked and turned off my headlights than the porch light came on and Bosco came running and barking from the house. I got out of my truck and ruffled his ears before going through the open gate and up the path to the front porch. It was less than three weeks till Christmas. Unlike nearly all of the other houses on my way here, the Bolanders had no colored lights, but I did not expect any. Through the picture window to the left of the door I could see that the tv was on. It looked like the weatherman at the station over in Billings was telling how cold it was going to be. Across from it, one of those deer antler lamps, not real big with a tan shade, sat on an end table next to an old green couch. It cast just enough light that I could see there was nobody in the room and then the door opened, just wide enough for Owen to stick his head out. He looked at me like I was so much nothingness and said, hatefully, "What do you want?"

Beyond him, I could hear cooking noises in the kitchen. I said, still standing on the porch with clouds of my breath defining the space between us, "I need to talk to your mother."

"Why?"

"It's about your dad."

"What about him?"

Abruptly, Owen leaned back and the door opened. Norma stood there, dressed not in the dark blue dress and high heels that she'd been wearing that day in front of the courthouse but clothes that said who she had become. She had on Levis with a small hole above the right knee that showed her long underwear and a long-sleeved brown flannel shirt with an insulated underwear top visible at her neck. She smelled of hay and from her cowboy boots, a hint of manure. Her eyes were sad, she said, "What's this about Fred?"

I sighed and shook my head. I said, "Norma, I'm sorry to have to tell you but Fred has been killed in a fight."

For a few seconds, she seemed paralyzed as shock and disbelief consumed her. In that painful silence, the tv weatherman way off in Billings, safe and secure, said like he could give a shit that Fred was dead, *folks, the low in Cutbank tonight is expected to be 32 below zero so bundle up-* And then Norma's knees started to buckle, and her hands went to her face as she began to wail, "No, no, this can't be."

Owen put his arm around his mother and helped her to the couch. I stepped inside and closed the door behind me so as to stop the invasion of the cold night air. I said, as much to justify my continued presence as it was to be sympathetic,

"The prison people were real short on details, just that Fred had been involved in a fight."

Norma looked up at me, she said with surprising clarity, "Fred never looked for trouble."

Little Freddy Bolander in his blue FFA jacket ran through my mind again as I said, "I know, Norma, but in prison trouble has a way of finding even those that don't want anything to do with it."

Owen said, almost shouting, "This is all that damned Stroud's fault. Dad and Teddy went out to Badger Creek that day to cut some posts, just minding their own business when they run into that set gun. And from what I hear, Stroud's never been charged with that. Why the hell is that? Cause he's got money? I wanna know."

I knew it was a sore spot with Cheevers, the fact that he couldn't make a case against Stroud for the set gun. But the old man that I had talked to at the Lumberjack about Stroud and Joe and the killing of bears had gotten a bad case of amnesia. I said, "The game department wants in the worst way to cite Stroud for that set gun, but they just don't have any solid proof."

Owen exploded. "Proof, my brother's laying dead down there in the cemetery. Ain't that proof enough?"

"Nobody but your dad saw the gun? And as you well know, it was gone when we went to look for it."

"Well, I heard you found it at the herder's camp."

"I think it was the same gun and you do too, but proving that to a judge and jury, or for that matter, getting the DA to even prosecute Stroud for it is another issue."

Owen scoffed. "Well, that pudgy little bastard didn't have any trouble making a case against my father." And then he added, "Maybe if you hadn't killed that other sheep herder, he would've spilled the beans on Stroud."

I frowned at Owen but said, "I'm sorry, Owen. I just don't think the judge believed your dad's story."

"Well, screw you and all them people in that courthouse. That sheepherder threw the first punch. He got what was coming to him."

I'd thought so many times about that day. In a way, it made sense to me that Fred, in spite of having his dead son in the back of his pickup, would have to be provoked into throwing the first punch. But when I put myself in his shoes and what I might have done, I tended to think the judge saw it as it really happened. However, there would be damned few people that I would ever tell that to and the Bolanders were not among them. I said, looking mostly at Norma, "The prison people said Fred's body could be picked up on Monday."

Norma looked at me, too overwhelmed by it all to say anything, but Owen blurted out. "The state took him over there so they can damned well bring him back. We're funeral poor. You know Reinecker ain't gonna drive all the way over to Deerlodge and back for free."

I nodded. "I know, Owen. I'll ask if the prison will bring your dad home, but I wouldn't get your hopes up."

Owen snorted in a sarcastic way. "You'll ask, I bet." He stood up. "I think it's time for you to go."

I hesitated, thinking there was something more that I should say, but what? My credibility with Owen was non-existent and Norma only slightly better. I started to open the door when Owen said, "Oh, Sheriff."

I turned to face him.

He smiled, "You have a Merry Christmas."

I said nothing and closed the door behind me.

It was difficult to not come away with some of the Bolander's sadness, even though the rest of the world seemed oblivious to it. The neighbors on the other side of Elk Creek and down the road a little way had a Christmas tree up. I could see it through their living room window. It had red, blue and green lights that alternately flashed. And my favorite radio station now played nothing but Christmas music. The radio announcer hyped Bing Crosby's *White Christmas* as an all-time people's favorite before playing it. I turned it up, trying to extract my mind from the Bolander's living room. But it did no good.

CHAPTER SEVENTEEN

I suspect it may have been because it was close to Christmas rather than anything I said, but the man in charge of such things at Deerlodge agreed to bring Fred home. I did not go back to the Bolander ranch to tell them, opting instead to just pass this on to the Reinecker funeral home. Fred's obituary, and the fact they had buried him on the eleventh of December, was in the paper. The write-up said nothing about him being in prison. It said instead that Fred had gone to be with his heavenly father. And so, it was just Owen and Norma out there on Elk Creek. I wondered how long they would make it with Owen being the pot head that he was. I could smell it on him that night mixed in with whatever it was Norma was cooking in the kitchen. But that may have been the least of their problems. They'd had to pay for two funerals, a bail bondsman, a lawyer, and they likely had a payment due at the bank. To their credit, the Mormon church held a benefit spaghetti dinner for Norma. Had things been different, we would have attended the dinner. I heard it made $142 or about two hours of Herb Boyer's time.

For us, Christmas seemed hollow without Phil and Roy. It was like we were in a bad dream and, at some point, we'd wake up and there they'd be, but obviously that never happened. On Christmas eve day it had started snowing around three o'clock in the afternoon. There were those people, I'm sure, who saw this as a good thing as they would now have a white Christmas. However, in our house nobody saw it that way. Snow on the roads, especially since it was the first significant snow of the season, meant there were bound to be wrecks and the possibility I would be called out. Speculation in this regard ended not long after the ten o'clock news had started. Dispatch called and requested that I respond to a rollover with injuries about three miles up Gold Creek. I hung up the phone and said to Ellen, Niko and Emma having gone to their rooms earlier, "I may be a while."

She smiled wryly, "Never fails."

I laughed. "That's why I get the big bucks."

And then we both laughed. She said, as I sat down in the chair across from the couch and pulled on my boots, "You want me to fix you a thermos of coffee?"

"No, thanks Hon, I need to go."

"Are you sure? Just take a minute to make some instant."

I stood up and started toward the utility room and my coat, hat and gun belt. I said over my shoulder, "Appreciate the offer but I better get on the road."

"Well, you be really careful. There must be eight or nine inches of snow. Hopefully, the snowplows will be out."

"Up Gold Creek?"

"You've got chains in your pickup, don't you?"

I smiled, "You know my philosophy about chains."

Ellen recited, "If it's bad enough for chains maybe you shouldn't be going there."

I looked at her and grinned, "Yeah, I've got chains." And then the kitchen phone began to ring. I brushed past Ellen. "I better get that. It might be the dispatch." On the third ring, I picked it up, "Hello."

"Hi Dad. Merry Christmas."

My heart sank. "Well, Merry Christmas to you. How are you?"

"I'm ok, wish I was home."

"We wish you were home too. I can hear music playing. Where are you?"

"The enlisted men's club. Not much else open on Pendleton and I think even it's going to close pretty soon."

I looked at Ellen and shook my head. I said to Roy, "Son, I've gotta turn you over to your mother. I was just on my way to a call.'

He hesitated only slightly, but said, his voice hinting at being slightly drunk, "Sure, Dad. You be careful."

"Call tomorrow, son, when we can talk. Call collect. Love you."

"Alright Dad. Love you."

I handed Ellen the phone and gave her a peck on the lips before going outside. It was still snowing. The porch light exaggerated its intensity but anyway you cut it, the snow was getting deeper. I sighed as I bent down and turned in the hubs on my pickup. I whispered, "Hell, I'm gonna have to leave outta my own yard in four-high."

And so, my night began. By the time I got to the Gold Creek Road turnoff I'd already been driving for several miles with my chains on. There was no way the ambulance was going to make it in to where the wreck was supposed to be. Dispatch said there were no snowplows available, at least not anytime soon. We had no choice but to leave the ambulance on the main road. One of the attendants rode in with me and the other with Dick McFarland in the Sinclair station's four-wheel drive wrecker that was chained up all the way around. The reporting party had driven out of Gold Creek and on down the main road a mile or so before coming to a ranch with a phone. They'd barely made it that far due to the snow, so they went on home confident that we were on the way. But by the time we got there, the people in the red Chevy pickup were dead. They were old but likely would've had some good life left. Their name was Markum, Lester and Dorothy. They lived at the head of Gold Creek, a nice place in the summer but not so much now. In the blinding snow they had simply driven off a curve in the gravel road and went over an embankment. Lester had been crushed in the cab of the pickup while Dorothy and their golden retriever had been thrown out. The dog survived. Tracks and blood around the vehicle suggested Dorothy had too. She died apparently trying to get Lester out. I took their dog, who appeared ok, to their daughter's place in town. It was a little after five when I knocked on the door and close to five-thirty when I'd told them all that I knew. It was gut wrenching to see little kids wake up expecting to see what Santa had brought them and instead seeing a stranger with a badge and gun telling them that grandpa and grandma were dead.

CHAPTER EIGHTEEN

It was a sunny day in the middle of March. Most everybody except hippy ski bums were glad to see the snow melted from the valley floor and gradually retreating up the sides of the mountains. Ellen and I were having lunch at the Coffee Cup when in walks Raymond O'Leary. I nodded a simple *hello* in his direction which he took as an invitation to come over to our table and sit down. There not having been any dead people turn up that required our collective attention for over two months I said, "Long time no see."

He played along with the tenor of how the winter had been, "Well, today is my first day out of hibernation."

Ellen and I laughed politely. I said, "So, how's business?"

He looked around to see who might be listening and then said, with a grin, "You know as long and dreary as this winter has been, I thought people would have died just to be free of it." And then he broke into a laugh.

I said, almost straight faced, "Lesser of two evils, I guess."

It appeared he was about to grace us with some more undertaker humor when the waitress, a dark-haired buxom girl in her mid-twenties, stopped at our table and set a glass of water in front of Raymond. Since we had already ordered, she looked straight at him, "What'll it be?"

For a few seconds he pretended to be thinking while his eyes roved over the young girl to the point she would've been justified in charging him for the privilege, finally he said, "What's your special?"

The waitress, whose name was Melanie, was not oblivious to Raymond mentally undressing her. She gestured, with some indifference, to the white erasure board just over her right shoulder. She said, "Meatloaf and everything else it says there."

Raymond's face turned a little red but then he recovered, "Oh, I'll have that." And then he laughed as she wrote it down. He said, not knowing to let well enough alone, "Yeah, if your board had been a snake, I'd be dead."

Melanie looked sideways at Raymond and kind of sneered, "Yeah, then you'd be planting yourself."

Undeterred, Raymond watched the tight curves of Melanie's butt until she went behind the counter and hung his ticket on the metal rack. She shouted, "Special."

I said, "So, how's business at the CO-OP?"

Raymond came back to where Ellen and I were. He said, "Good, sold lots of trough heaters and supplement block this winter."

I said, since it'd been a nagging curiosity of mine from that night when I'd been there, "You see much of the Bolanders?"

"Not much, their credit's not good."

Ellen said, like she needed to defend them, "Well is it any wonder?"

Raymond said, "I've heard Norma looks bad."

I said, "Looks bad?"

"Tired and run down."

"It is calving season. That'll wear anybody out."

"I heard too that her son ain't worth much."

My mind went to Owen being a pothead. I knew from my experience as a young man out in the Gros Ventre valley that tending to calving cows 24 hours a day can take a lot out of a person. I didn't have any experience with the smoking dope part but I was guessing that it wouldn't help. I said, "That's too bad."

And then one of those awkward moments where nobody has anything to say descended upon the table. It grew as we sat there looking at one another and listening to the din of lunch time patrons talking and laughing, plates clanging in the kitchen and the cook occasionally hollering, *order up.* Raymond quickly took a drink of water as if to volley the obligation to speak back to our side of the table. Ellen said, "It sure is nice out and spring is still two days away."

Before I could add what I knew about the upcoming weather, Raymond came to life, he said, "I saw in the paper where your son graduated from Marine boot camp."

I said, "Yeah, last fall. He's coming home next week on leave."

Raymond said, "Is he going to Vietnam? Seems like they all are. My cousin did. He was in the Army."

I'd purposely stopped short of mentioning that Roy had orders for Vietnam as discussing the war upset Ellen. She still believed that, had Roy joined the Air Force, he could've gotten assigned to the base up at Great Falls. I tried to tell her that the Air Force sent people to Vietnam too but, of course, that didn't help. I said to Raymond, "Yeah, he's going to Vietnam."

"What's his job?"

I could feel Ellen's uneasiness. I said, "Infantry."

Raymond instantly cringed and shook his head, "Well, I guess that's what Marines do. My cousin, the one that was in the Army, he was in the infantry. He tripped some kind of booby-trap. Blew his legs off from the knees down. He-"

Ellen abruptly slid her chair back, she said, her voice beginning to falter, "Excuse me." And then she walked away towards the rest room.

It now dawned on Raymond that he'd screwed up, he said, "I'm sorry, sometimes I just don't think."

I sighed. "Ellen doesn't do well with war talk. She won't even watch the news anymore."

"I'm sorry, I'll tell her that I am when she comes back."

"No, Raymond, just drop it."

And so we did, talking about how good the meatloaf was and the fact spring was surely here as I'd seen red-wing blackbirds out in the county over two weeks ago.

CHAPTER NINETEEN

Ellen was smiling broadly. "I can't believe he's finally coming home. It seems like he's been gone forever."

I looked up from the sourdough hotcake that I was carving a bite out of, "Been almost seven months but I bet to Roy, it seems like seven years."

"It's going to be fun, Andy. We'll pick up Roy and then, like we talked, have an early dinner at the Cattlemen's Club. Roy's looking forward to it."

"Oh, I know he is. It's his favorite place to eat, mine too as far as that goes."

I saw Ellen's eyes go up to the clock on the wall, it read, 8:45. She said, "What time do you think we should leave?"

I said, "Well, his plane gets in at 2:15. It's two hours to Great Falls so I figure if we've got wheels rolling by eleven, we'll be good."

"What if we have a flat? Maybe we should leave a little sooner."

I grinned. "Ok, 10:45."

"I don't mean to be a nervous Nellie, it's just I've missed him so much."

"I have too."

"But I think you handle it better than I do."

I shrugged and took a drink of my coffee.

Ellen slid her hand across the table to mine. She said, "I didn't mean for it to sound like a contest."

"I know, I didn't take it that way"

Still holding my hand, she said, "I love you."

I said, just as Emma came around the corner, "I love you too."

Emma laughed. "Should I come back later?"

Before I could come up with something smart to say the phone began to ring. Emma answered it, "Yarnell residence," and then she looked at me, "It's Sharon at the dispatch."

Ellen said, the concern clearly evident in her voice, "Andy, it's Saturday. You already told them you were going out of town."

I took the phone. "Good morning, Sharon."

She cut right to it. "Sorry to bother you Andy, but Tyler wanted me to call you. Says he stumbled on to what looks like a murder."

"A murder, where at?"

"Out in the Gros Ventre valley near a forest service campground called Cottonwood Crossing. He said you'd know where it's at."

From the corner of my eye, I could see that both Ellen and Emma were listening intently. I said, "Does he know who the victim is?"

"Yes, you know him too. It's that Stroud kid."

I blurted out, "Holy shit, pardon my French, Sharon."

"No problem, that was kinda my reaction when I first heard it. I guess that's why Tyler thought you should know."

"Yeah, Billy's father is going to want answers pronto. But I guess any parent would."

"What should I tell Tyler?"

I looked over at Ellen and shook my head. "Tell him I'm on my way. And say, have you called O'Leary?"

"Yes, he's headed out there now."

"Alright, thanks, Sharon."

I'd barely hung up the phone when Ellen said, "Dammit, Andy, can't this family ever complete anything we've got planned without your job interfering?"

I looked at her. She was clearly upset. Her patience for these disruptions to our life had gotten to be less and less over the past year. I said, "Tyler needs me. You know how Orville Stroud is. There can't be any missed steps here. I'm sorry."

Ellen frowned and shook her head. "Alright, I guess it'll just be me, Emma and Bella."

"You'll be ok."

She said in an overly emphatic voice, "I know that Andy, but it would just be nice to do this as a family."

"I agree, but we can't. Tell Roy I'm sorry that I couldn't be there. Tell him we'll all go to Buckhorn Lake while he's home for a picnic and fishing."

Ellen scoffed, "Oh, you think you can find the time?"

I sighed and shook my head. "I need to change clothes."

It took me less than five minutes to get ready to go. When I came out of the bedroom, I found Ellen sitting on the living room couch with a cup of coffee. I'd assumed, or hoped, that while I had been gone she would have come around to seeing things differently but she said, "You know, Andy, maybe you should consider retiring this year."

Her words caught me off guard. I didn't need this, not now. I flashed a brief, but angry look at her, I said, "And do what, Ellen, sell used cars? Be Raymond's assistant at the CO-OP?"

"It'd be seasonal but maybe you could get on as a maintenance worker with the forest service."

I looked at her, my mind having gone back to the other times over the past several years that we'd had this discussion with the same conclusion. I said, "Maybe we can talk tonight."

"Andy, I'm serious about this."

"I've got to go." And with that I walked out and started my truck up Yellow Dog Road. My departure had been hurtful to me, and I suspect Ellen too. In all our years of being married, I could count on one hand and still have two or three fingers left over, the times, when parting, that we hadn't kissed and told one another, *I love you.*

I pushed my old pickup hard, doing 80-85 mph when the road allowed, all the way until I came to the cemetery just south of Cedarville. I'd noted my gas gauge when I left home and had decided at the time that I would get gas out in the Gros Ventre. It'd been dry enough lately and my speed was such that the dust boiled up around my wheels as I came off the pavement and across the graveled area in front of the Cedarville store. Not long after I started pumping my gas, I heard the store owner's voice behind me. "What's all the hu-bub about? I saw the hearse go by a little while ago."

I turned sideways to my truck and looked over. "I'm not at liberty to say just yet, Ralph."

"Somebody die?"

I glanced at Ralph and then the meter on the pump, it was scrolling by 5.2 gallons. I had less than a quarter tank, meaning that I had another 10 or 11 gallons of questioning to go.

Ralph said, "Yeah, that O'Leary kid went sailing through here about 20 minutes ago. I'll tell ya, he wasn't lettin' any grass grow under it. No excuse for driving that fast. You see how many pitch players and coffee drinkers there are over at the Lumberjack. Ever one of them pickups over there has got a dog or two with it. You never know when one of 'em is gonna come trottin' out on the road."

I said, "I'll tell O'Leary to slow down coming through here."

"So, you're meeting up with him?"

I couldn't help but grin. "Yeah, Ralph. I am, but that's all I can tell you."

"Oh, I know you got to notify the next of kin and all that before you can tell anyone else. I get it. I sure wouldn't want to hear about one of my family being dead from some Joe Blow."

I was about to try and steer Ralph onto a different topic when, from the corner of my eye, I caught sight of a blue pickup coming into town from the north. Inwardly, I said to myself, *Oh shit, not here, not now.* But on he came, past the Lumberjack, past the Antler until finally stopping straight across from me on the other side of the pumps. I put on a serious face and looked straight at Ralph. I said in a low voice, "I'm gonna need some time alone with Stroud."

A sudden awareness came over Ralph's face like I'd just given him a big clue to the riddle he'd been trying to solve. He said, "Sure, Andy," and began walking quickly back to the store, giving Orville a quick casual wave.

Stroud opened his door and got out, purposely not looking at me. He was about to round the corner at the front of his pickup and go into the store when I said, "Mr. Stroud, I need to talk with you."

He stopped and looked back at me like he didn't have time for this, he said, his tone curt and unfriendly, "About what?"

I could see Ralph had been joined by his wife at the window, apparently unashamed to be voyeurs of another man's grief. My heart had begun to hammer the moment I saw Stroud's pickup coming into town. I hated having to do this, even to Stroud, I said, "Orville, I'm afraid I've got some bad news for you."

His face instantly became fearful, almost like he was going to be sick, he shot back, his voice weak, "About Billy, he didn't come home last night but he sometimes does that. What has that kid done now? Have you got him in jail?"

I've been told my face is like an open book. Before I could tell him, Stroud had read what was there. Beneath the brim of his clean gray Stetson, I could see that his eyes had watered up, he said, his voice about to break, "He's dead, isn't he?"

I nodded. "Yeah, he is."

"Was it a wreck? I told him that damned hot rod car would get him killed, but he had to have it."

I shook my head. "No, it looks like somebody murdered him."

Unlike what I expected, Stroud did not react with shock or surprise. Instead for a few seconds he was quiet, his mind having gone off somewhere else. And then he came back, "How was he killed?"

"I don't know. I'm on my way there now."

"There?"

"Cottonwood Crossing campground."

"The kids party there a lot."

"I'm aware of that, but they usually don't go there until summer."

And then Stroud's demeanor became more vengeful than sad, he said, "You know that damned Bolander kid, the one that's been to Vietnam, you may want to look him up. Him and Billy got into a scrap last winter."

"Well, we'll have to see where the evidence takes us."

"It's not rocket science, Sheriff. Owen Bolander blames me for his father and brother being dead."

I couldn't help but hesitate. Stroud was looking at me like he expected me to take his side, but I'd laid awake too many nights thinking how everybody's lives would be better if only Joe Garmendia hadn't put out that set gun. Teddy and Fred and Felipe and Joe and even Phil, they'd all be alive if Stroud hadn't taken it upon himself to rid the mountains of bears. My heart hammered a little harder. I said, him being a grieving parent or not, "Well, Orville, it was your set gun that started all of that trouble."

He glared at me and then snorted defiantly, "Like I've already told you in the past, I had nothing to do with the set gun that killed that Bolander kid."

I nodded. "Alright, Orville, I didn't mean to plow that field again. For now, though, I'd suggest you go on home. I'll come by there after we've processed the crime scene."

Stroud shouted, "No, I ain't going home. I want to see what happened to my boy."

"I can see why you'd want to. But having done this for over 20 years I can tell you, as a parent, I'd rather remember my boy as he was and not how he might look today. Please, Orville, go on home. Your family is going to need you. I promise, I'll come by later."

It may have been that I'd shown Orville just enough compassion to cause his stoic façade to crumble but, whatever the reason, he appeared to stagger slightly. He placed his left hand on the hood of his pickup to catch himself.

Through the store window I could see Ralph's wife take a tissue from her apron pocket and dab at her nose. They saw that I saw them, but they did not turn away. I stepped close to Stroud, not certain if I should, but I put my hand on his shoulder, I said, "Would you like for me to take you home?" Beyond him, in the store window, I could see that Ralph was pointing and saying something to his wife. Stroud took a deep breath and exhaled slowly as he shook his head, he said, his eyes a little more watery now, "No, I'll go on my own but you will come by later?"

"Yes, just as soon as I can."

He nodded, "Alright." And then he climbed into his pickup, pulled on past the pumps and headed back in the direction from which he'd come. He wasn't out of sight when Ralph came out of the store. He said, "That Stroud outfit is a magnet for death."

I nodded as I took the nozzle out of my tank and re-placed it in the side of the pump. I said only, "Yeah, they seem to be."

"Was this about that kid of his?"

"Yeah, it was." And then I added, figuring that Ralph would assume I was free to tell him now, "appears somebody killed him."

"Killed him?"

"That's all I can say, Ralph."

"Well, it doesn't surprise me. That little shit was a real hellion. Why, I've seen him go through town here I'll betcha 70 miles an hour."

At the risk of priming the rumor mill pump, I said, "You ever see Owen Bolander out here?"

"Yeah, every now and again."

"When was the last time you saw him?"

Ralph paused and looked over at the Antler Bar next door, I assumed to see if anyone was outside, satisfied that they weren't, he said, "Bolander was at the Antler yesterday afternoon for quite a while."

"I don't think he's of age."

Ralph grinned, "The way they see it in there if you're old enough to get drafted and go to Vietnam you're old enough to drink."

"You didn't hear it from me, but I tend to agree. Do you happen to recall what time Bolander left the Antler?"

"All I know is when I was closing up around eight that old pickup of his dad's was gone."

"Alright, thanks, Ralph."

"You think he's got something to do with this?"

I frowned slightly and said to myself, *Well, shit, here we go. This is all Norma needs is for word to get back to her that I'm investigating her son as a murder suspect.* I said to Ralph, "I'd appreciate it if you'd just keep this under your hat."

He said, "Oh sure, Andy, I will." But I knew as soon as he got back in the store Agnes would know everything that he did and would not be bound by any promise to keep quiet, which was pretty much an impossibility for her anyway.

About seven miles north of Cedarville, I turned west off of CR29 onto a dirt road. It meandered for a couple of miles through mostly hayfields before going past a sign announcing you were on national forest land until finally ending at Cottonwood Creek. I was almost to the campground when my deputy came up on our tactical frequency wanting to know my location. I keyed my radio, "I'm just coming to the campground, where are you?"

"Go north along the creek about a half mile. You can't miss us."

"Copy, be there in a minute."

The campground was a mess. It reflected the aftermath of a wild drinking party. I paused momentarily to take stock of it. There were empty beer cans and bottles scattered over a wide area. Dark green wine bottles, mostly T.J. Swan, were abundant as well. Cardboard beer cases, six pack holders, potato chip bags and a white bra that somebody had purposely hung from the lower limb of a tree were also visible. A wispy column of smoke was trailing up from the end of a dead tree that was lying partially in a rock fire ring. The thinking, I suppose, was to just shove a little more of the tree into the ring as it was needed. The tree was about eight or nine inches in diameter and probably fifteen feet long. It didn't look like it would make a very good fire. Nonetheless, I turned my pickup off and got the shovel out of the bed. All around the cobble rock fire ring was short green grass and bare dirt that had been packed down by all of the foot and vehicle traffic. The chances of the smoldering embers going anywhere at this time of year were probably not great, but my time fighting fire for the forest service twenty some years ago wouldn't let me leave it as it was. It also appeared that somebody had attempted to feed the fire with household garbage as there were empty Campbell's soup cans, a Meadow Gold milk carton, some potato peelings and several magazines. I had just started scraping the glowing embers from the end of the log and mixing them with fresh dirt when my shovel turned over part of a magazine that hadn't burned to ash. Right there, on what appeared to have been a copy of Popular Mechanics, was a scorched but legible address label, it read: Bernie Schultz, General Delivery, Cedarville, MT. I reached down and carefully pulled the unburned label away from the brittle charcoal remains of the magazine cover. I put it between the pages of my notebook and tucked that back in my shirt pocket. It came as no surprise to me to see Bernie's trash here as I had history with him, and none of it was good. As a teenager he had purposely tried to run over their neighbor's dog, and in the process, got his butt whipped by an old man. This was one of the first disputes that I'd had to settle as a new deputy. It appeared that, all these years later, I would be going back to the Schultz place. After thoroughly scraping the end of the log I lifted it out of the ring and laid it on a patch of bare ground. I was about to get in my pickup when I heard Tyler come over the radio, "Yarnell – Cummins." I reached in and grabbed the mic. "Be there in a second, Tyler."

He came back, "Copy."

I idled on past several more fire rings that showed evidence of having been used last night, some picnic tables, and an outhouse before finally coming to the far end of the campground where a narrow dirt road took off up along the creek. The road was just two tracks with a high ridge in the middle that I envisioned Billy's GTO dragging bottom, if that's how he got here. Along the creek were willows, sagebrush, and cottonwood trees that had not yet acquired a new crop of leaves. In a few minutes, I came into a clearing where people had camped at one time and Billy now lay dead. I parked next to the hearse and well short of the yellow crime scene tape that Tyler had strung up. I'd barely got out of my truck when Tyler called out, "Thought maybe you got lost."

"Well, I stopped at the new Gros Ventre valley junk yard, put out a little fire and collected some evidence, so I been busy."

A sheepish look came over Tyler's face that was vaguely disguised by his dark moustache as he looked over at Raymond. Before he could say anything, Raymond said, "I told you there was some litter down there."

I said to Tyler as I stepped over the yellow tape, "How'd you get here?"

He said, trying to sound like it was perfectly logical, "I crossed the crick up at Buck Canyon and came down along it."

Had it not been for the fact that Billy was laying there dead in the dirt, I would have laughed and called Tyler on his obvious scouting the creek to see if the water was down enough for the fishing to be good, but I said, "Those damned kids trashed the campground. That's where they had their party. So, I guess the 64 dollar question is, why was Billy Stroud up here?"

Raymond threw in, "It appears he got in a fight with somebody and they got the better of him."

I walked over to where Billy was laying and knelt beside him. There was a cut over his right eye that had bled down into the socket below. Still, both of his eyes were wide open staring straight up at some puffy white clouds lost in a sea of blue. He'd bled a lot too, from his nose and several open cuts on his lips where they'd been crushed into his teeth. His appearance reminded me of how I'd looked after my fight with Joe Garmendia. And then, in the next instant, the roar of my.38 exploded in my mind and I felt the sudden weight of Joe upon me and him gasping, struggling to live and then he just sighed and it was over, at least that part of it was. I said, "Look at his hands. It must have been a one-sided fight. They haven't got a mark on them."

Raymond said, "Look at his throat. He's got a nasty bruise there and it looks like there may be some internal distention."

I said, "Maybe he was punched hard, real hard in the throat."

Tyler knelt beside me and said, "I was into Tae Kwon Do for a little while and that was one of the places they said you should hit somebody if you wanted to disable them. They said your goal wasn't to just make contact with your opponent's throat, but that you should visualize punching through it to a point beyond it." And then he made a fist with his right hand and drew it back along his side, but chest high, and fired it straight out a couple of times to demonstrate. He added, "I never got beyond a yellow belt, but somebody with a black belt against a regular person could really mess them up."

I nodded, "I imagine they could, but so could a good bar room fighter. Billy's gonna need an autopsy."

Raymond, who was still standing and looking down at us, said, "It'd probably be best if I take him to Helena for a full work up. The inside of his car reeks of marijuana and there is a half empty bottle of wine and a pint of Jack Daniels that's nearly gone."

I said, "Yeah, I imagine Billy's toxicology report could make for some interesting reading." I stood up as did Tyler. I looked around. The clearing was about the size of a lot for a small house. A carpet of green grass, about bite-high, was struggling to grow amongst the cow pies. Billy had pulled his GTO off the road, nose in to a couple of young cottonwood trees. I walked over to it and looked inside. The car was as cluttered as the day I arrested him in town. I roved my eyes over the car's interior looking for anything that Tyler or Raymond might have missed. And then my focus stalled on the keys in the ignition, they were in the, on, position. I looked at the gas gauge. The needle lay flat. I said, "Looks like the battery's dead. Billy was probably sitting here, listening to the radio, waiting for somebody."

"But why come away from the party?" said Tyler. "I mean if he wanted to sell somebody some pot, I would think in the dark and drunkenness of the party he could have done that without anybody being the wiser."

Raymond added his speculation, "Maybe he was meeting a girl?"

I shook my head. "Why wouldn't she just ride up here with him? I mean, if she's that ashamed to be seen with him surely she's smart enough to figure out that the other party-goers will notice that she's gone, and Billy too and connect the dots."

Tyler said, "But what if they said they were going home?"

"What girl goes to a party by herself?" And then I added, "We need to dust the inside of this car for prints. Hopefully, Billy's killer got in the car for a while."

Tyler started walking towards his car. He said over his shoulder, "I'll get my kit."

Raymond said, "You suppose we can load Billy now?"

I scrunched my face up in uncertainty and shook my head slightly, "No, not just yet. Let's go over everything inside the tape. There might be something that'll jump out at us. How about you take what's to the left of the road and I'll take the right. It'll be kind of a two-man grid, cover it real good."

"Alright, Andy."

I gave Raymond the side of the road where the GTO was parked. I took the side where Billy was laying. Beginning at the intersection of the tape and the edge of the road, I started walking back and forth in a straight line between the boundaries of the tape. Each swath was about 40 paces long. As I walked this imaginary line, I scanned the ground for about five or six feet to either side of it. But, with the meadow grass being more like a putting green splattered with cow shit, I wasn't coming up with much. And then, when I was on my next to last swath, I saw a footprint in the fresh dirt that a mole had pushed up. The print was unique in that between the ball of the foot and the heel there was a rectangular imprint. What was in the imprint I could not tell, but it was a fresh track and worthy of preserving. I walked back to where Raymond was. I said, "Hold up one of your feet so I can see the bottom of your shoe."

He gave me a puzzled look but did as I asked. The track wasn't his. I hollered at Tyler, "Do the soles of your boots have a rectangle on them. He said, "Damned if I know." And then he got out of Billy's car and stood on one foot while looking at the bottom of the other." He shouted, "Nope, they're just plain."

"I'm gonna flag a footprint over here that I think we need to cast and photograph." I then went to my pickup and got a bright red pin flag, my camera, and casting materials out of a locked storage box in its bed. The one thing I was lacking was water so, after marking the footprint's location with the flag, I took the bowl for mixing the plaster over to the creek, which was just outside of the yellow tape. I'd no sooner brushed past some willows near the edge of the water when I spotted in the soft mud two more of the same tracks as in the clearing. I froze where I was and tried to visualize why this person would stand almost in the water. And then, the rolodex of bad memories in my mind flopped open to how bloody and swollen Fred's knuckles had looked. I thought, *Maybe the killer came over here to wash the blood off of his hands?*

By the time we'd finished at the crime scene it was close to three o'clock. Raymond headed to town with Billy, Tyler waited for the Sinclair's wrecker to come from Fremont and tow Billy's car, and Ellen, Emma and Bella had likely picked up Roy and were on their way to the Cattlemen's Club for a steak dinner. I, on the other hand, started for the Stroud ranch. To say that I was not looking forward to explaining to grieving parents how their son had died was an understatement. Over the years, I had done many death notifications and they never got easier. Each one left a scar that has randomly peppered my dreams. Today would be another one.

Stroud's pickup was parked on the cement driveway in front of his garage. A split rail fence that was stained the same dark color as their log house surrounded the front yard. Its purpose was entirely aesthetic as it was comprised of just two rails, barely crotch high to a normal person. I parked on the bare dirt just outside the fence and started up the flagstone walkway that ran through the lush green lawn. I thought it strange that there was no dog to greet me. Almost everybody in the Gros Ventre had a dog or two but, apparently, not the Strouds. I knocked on the door with its over-sized black door handle, momentarily it opened and Orville stood before me. He said, "I thought maybe you weren't coming."

Beyond him, in an elegant high ceiling living room, I could see a middle-aged woman with strawberry blonde hair dressed in jeans and a tie-died tee shirt sitting next to a teenage girl that resembled her. They were together on a big brown leather couch. I said, "An investigation takes time. I wanted to be sure we didn't miss anything."

"So, what did you find out?"

From behind Stroud, his wife called out, "Dammit, Orville, invite him in. We want to hear too."

Orville stepped to the side. "Come in, Sheriff."

I closed the door behind me and followed Stroud into the room. He paused near a padded leather chair across from the couch and a dark hickory wood coffee table on black iron wheels and gestured, "Have a seat."

I sat down while Stroud took up a mixed drink from an end table next to another padded chair straight across from me. He took a seat on the hearth of a huge rock fireplace to my right. Ironically, there was a grizzly bear rug hanging on the wall to the left of the fireplace chimney. I couldn't help but wonder if it had been killed by one of his set guns. He said, "What can you tell us?"

"It appears that Billy died as the result of a fight about a half mile north of the Cottonwood campground. We think he may have been waiting at that spot for someone, maybe the person who killed him."

Stroud took a sip of his drink. "That's it."

"For now, it is. We've collected some fingerprints and a cast of a shoe print. And we've towed Billy's car to town. We'll go through it again and then maybe when we get the autopsy results back, we'll know more about how he died."

Mrs. Stroud grimaced. Her eyes were red but she was not crying now, she said, "Is that necessary?"

I looked over at her. A large colorful tapestry hung on the wall behind her. It depicted a herd of sheep in a mountain meadow. I said, "I'm sorry, but in cases where we're almost certain that foul play is involved an autopsy is required."

She sighed. "I just didn't want to see my boy cut up like that." And then the ice cubes in her glass rattled as she put it to her mouth and tilted it up.

Orville said, his voice no longer civil, "I'm tellin' ya, you need to go talk to that Bolander kid. He's got it out for me and Billy. Hell, him just back from the war, killing would come easy to him. If you don't talk to him I will, cuz I'm not shy about such things."

"Hold on, Orville. I don't think it's a good idea for you to approach Owen Bolander. I'll talk to him and let you know what he has to say."

Mrs. Stroud said, while holding her empty glass, "Orville, give the man some time."

Stroud glared at his wife, he said, "I can't feature anybody else wanting to kill Billy, can you?"

I said, "From the looks of that campground, there were a lot of people out there last night and a lot of drinking going on. Too much liquor can make people do things that you might never expect."

Orville said, "I agree, but murder? My boy?"

"It might not have been intentional, just a fight that got out of hand. Based on the injury to Billy's neck we're speculating that maybe he tangled with somebody that was into martial arts."

From the corner of my eye I could see Stroud's daughter suddenly come alive. She said, "You think it was somebody that was into karate that killed Billy?"

I looked at the girl. "That was just my deputy brainstorming. It could just as easily have been a good bar room brawler. We really don't know."

The sudden rigidness that had come to the girl's face slowly began to drain away. She said, "Oh, Billy wasn't much of a fighter."

It flashed in my mind, that for not being a fighter, Billy ran his mouth too much. I said, "There were too many people at this party for us to not figure this out."

The girl said, "I hope so. Billy was wild but he didn't deserve this."

I stood up. "Well, I guess I better be going. I've got some other stops to make."

Orville said curtly, "They got to do with Billy?"

"Yes, but I'd rather not say anything more at this point."

"I thought you were going to be open about all of this."

"I will be when I have something solid."

Stroud snorted, "Well, we'll see, but just so you know, my patience is not unlimited."

"I understand."

CHAPTER TWENTY

B ernie Schultz inherited the family ranch about five years ago after his father had a stroke while cutting hay. He'd pitched forward out of the swather's seat and fell down onto the sickle bar and beneath the big paddle reel. He was cut and thrashed unmercifully until the out of control machine ran into a barbed wire fence and died. Naturally, of course, I'd been called to the scene by Bernie. It was not a pretty sight, but it is one that, far too often, comes to mind when I happen to see a swather, especially a John Deere. This was the last time that I'd had occasion to talk to Bernie. It wasn't that I hadn't seen him in town, it was more that I just didn't care for the guy. I suspected that feeling was mutual. Some years ago, when Bernie's father was still alive, I had stopped at the Lumberjack for a cup of coffee and to catch up on any scuttlebutt in the valley that a sheriff should know about. It was while I was sitting at the counter drinking my coffee and shooting the breeze with the café owner that Bernie's name came up at the round table to the left of me. There were four or five guys playing penny ante pitch. For a few minutes, the conversation turned to Bernie's work ethic. None of what was said was very complimentary but the one comment I do recall was, *that kid is about one peg above tits on a boar.* So, it came as no surprise to me when I pulled up in front of Bernie's single wide trailer that there were four vehicles parked in front of it. One was on blocks and another had the hood up. As I got out of my pickup, a brown dog with tangled and matted hair came out from beneath the trailer's rickety wooden steps and began to bark. There was no yard, just hard-packed dirt except where the dog had dug a hole. I started through the clutter. There were several used tires, a shovel, bucket, a bicycle with only one wheel, empty cans and bottles, a green fifty gallon barrel with a red hand pump and lots of dog shit. I was nearly to the steps when I stopped to make friends with the snarling dog and the trailer door opened. Bernie stepped out onto the landing, which was about four feet square. He was in his stocking feet and wearing a dirty white tee shirt that didn't quite conceal that part of his belly hanging over his Levis. His dark hair looked as if it had been combed with an egg beater. He said, "What can I do for ya, Sheriff?"

I said, "Well, there was a wild drinking party over at the Cottonwood campground last night. I found some of your trash there. So, I naturally assumed you were there?"

Bernie frowned angrily and looked back inside, he shouted, "Robby, get yer ass out here."

I could hear the tv playing and then the sound of rapid and heavy footsteps coming from further back in the trailer followed by a teenage boy abruptly filling the doorway. He was skinny with red hair and freckles. Momentarily, the source of those genes appeared behind him but she kept quiet. Robby's eyes got big as he looked down at where I was standing. Bernie said to him, "Did you go to that beer bust last night at the Cottonwood campground?"

Robby had that, *deer in the headlights look*. It was clear he was struggling with what to say but finally, he said, "Yeah, I was there for a little while but I just had a couple of Cokes."

I laughed and said sarcastically, "Well, you must have taken that trash with you because I didn't see any Coke cans out there. It's too bad you didn't take the rest of what you tried to burn."

He came back, "I don't see the problem. I threw it in the fire."

"Cans don't burn, neither did some of the other crap you threw in there. But look, here's the deal. I won't ticket you for littering if you agree to clean up the trash at the campground."

"All of it?"

"Yup, or you pay the fine and clean up just what's yours in the fire ring."

"But I didn't put all that other stuff out there."

"I know, so suppose you tell me about a couple of people that I'm interested in."

"Who's that?"

"Billy Stroud and Owen Bolander, did you see them interact in any way?"

Robby snorted. "Yeah, a lot of people did. They got into a shoving match by one of the fires but people broke them up before it got very far."

"What time was that?"

"I don't know. I don't wear a watch, but I'm guessing around seven o'clock. It was just starting to get dark."

"What about later? Did you see where they went?"

Robby scoffed. "Wasn't my job to watch 'em."

From behind him, his mother said, "Don't be a smartass."

Bernie said, "Why are you interested in these two guys?"

I said, "Somebody killed Billy Stroud last night."

"Ho-lee shit, so you think it was that crazy Bolander kid that did it?"

I shrugged. "I don't know anything for sure. I'm just trying to follow up on rumors I've heard."

"Well, everybody knows there's bad blood between the Bolanders and Orville Stroud."

I said to Robby, "I'm gonna need a list of everybody at the party and I want it by Monday because I intend on coming to the school and interviewing people."

Mild shock, then indignation came over his face, he said, "No, if I do this my name will be mud. There's probably even a few guys that will want to whip my ass for squealing on them."

"I've got to clear this with your principle but I'm guessing it won't be a problem. I'll see you around ten."

And then Robby laughed in a wry sort of way, he said, "Alright, I'll have your list come Monday morning."

Robby's sudden smugness made me a little uneasy, but I let it go and said, "Thank you, I'll see you Monday."

The drive back to town gave me plenty of time to weigh the pros and cons of just going on home to see Roy and waiting until tomorrow to question Owen about the party. I'd nearly convinced myself that this course of action would be ok but when I got to town something in my conscience told me to continue on to the Bolander's. As I drove past the Sinclair, I could see Billy's GTO sitting in the fenced compound out back. It was a flashy car for Fremont and I knew that the speculation as to why it was behind the Sinclair had probably already begun. But that would just be among those who hadn't gotten the scoop from Dick McFarland, who had towed it. They would know Billy was dead and who knows if Dick had offered up Owen as the prime suspect. No, I needed to stay ahead of the rumor mill.

At about a quarter till seven, I once again bounced over the loose plank in the bridge down from the Bolander's house. Their lights were on as the canyon was in total shadow. Bosco was standing in the front yard, barking excitedly. I'd barely stopped my pickup when Owen came out onto the porch. I wondered if he'd been expecting me and I wondered too if I should have had the dispatch call Tyler at home and have him meet me here. But I knew doing that would have spoiled his going to the show tonight with his girl, so I did not. Hopefully, Owen was not another Joe Garmendia. Bosco followed me, still barking, to just short of the porch.

Owen went first, "I know why you're here."

"And why's that?"

"I saw that Stroud kid's car behind the Sinclair. I know he's dead."

I cut to it, "Well, do you know anything about how he got that way?"

Owen laughed in a mocking way. "You know, I'd actually thought that if something ever happened to that worthless little bastard, you'd probably come look me up and sure as shit, here you are."

"What I heard is you and Billy had words last night at that party out in the Gros Ventre. Any truth to that?"

"Yeah, we had a disagreement. I would have whipped his ass if people hadn't stepped in."

"What was this about?"

"Mostly him."

"You wanted to whip his ass just because he is who he is?"

Owen grinned and scoffed. "Pretty much."

"And there was nothing else that motivated you to want to do this?"

Anger flared in Owen's eyes. "What do you want me to say? That I killed him to get back at his old man because he killed my father and brother. Trust me, I've thought about doing that more than once, but if I'm going to throw my life away it'll be because I've killed Orville. That self-righteous sonovabitch is the one who needs to die."

The door quietly opened behind Owen and Norma stepped out beside him. She gently touched his left shoulder and said in a soft voice, "Don't be this way, Owen. It won't help."

He looked over at his mother. "What will help?"

Tears had come to Norma's eyes. She shook her head. "Your dad wouldn't want this."

I said, "Did you notice anybody else at the party that might have had it out for Billy?"

For a moment, it was clear that Owen was undecided if he should say what he was thinking but then he did, "At one point, I saw the Stroud kid having what appeared to be a pretty intense conversation with this guy that goes by the name of Jericho."

"Could you hear what they were talking about?"

"No, but I've heard that Jericho is the guy to talk to if a person wants to buy some weed."

My mind instantly reverted to what Dick at the Sinclair had told me about Owen wanting him to get high, but I didn't go there, I said, "This Jericho guy got a last name?"

Owen snickered, "Probably, but he's one of these flower child types that goes by one name."

"What does he look like?"

"Just another greasy long hair."

I frowned, "Could you be a little more specific?"

"Oh, I don't know, medium height but skinny. He's got long dishwater blonde hair down past his shoulders. He likes to wear peace symbol shit."

"You know where he lives?"

Owen shook his head. "Nope, he's pretty secretive about that."

"So, you know him?"

Owen grinned wryly, "Well, aren't you the detective."

I said, "I know you smoke dope, but this isn't about that."

"Like I said, I don't know where this guy lives."

"Do you know what he drives?"

"Yeah, he's got an old blue Ford van."

"Anything unusual about it?"

"Well, he's painted peace symbols on both sides of it."

"Does he have a job?"

Owen laughed, "He sells product."

I nodded and then briefly laughed along. I couldn't help but question if I'd spent a year in Vietnam and came home to the violent deaths of my brother and father if I might smoke dope too. I said, "Thanks for your help, Owen. I may contact you again, I'm not sure."

He said, his voice cold and abrupt, "Well, you know where to find me." And with that he and Norma went inside.

On the way back to town I pondered all that Owen had told me. I wanted to believe that he was innocent of killing Billy and that he was trying to be helpful. But, on the other hand, he could be a really good liar.

I knew as soon as I pulled up in front of our house that Roy wasn't there, his car was gone. Ellen met me in the kitchen and gave me a kiss. "You just missed everybody."

Everybody?"

"Roy went to see that Clark girl. I guess they've been writing back and forth. Emma is out with her friends and mom went back to her place."

"She getting settled in?"

"I guess. but the loneliness is no better."

"As many hours as she works, you'd think she wouldn't have time to be lonely."

Ellen stepped back from me slightly as if she had to position herself to say what she was about to. She said, looking right into my eyes, "I guess my dad is lucky to be dead, otherwise he'd be the lonely one."

I said, "Give me a break. I couldn't help being gone today."

Ellen sighed heavily. "I know, I'm sorry. It's just that your job seems to come before everything."

"How was Roy with my not coming today?"

"He said he was ok with it, but a little later he made a point of saying how it was too bad we couldn't make it to his boot camp graduation."

"I didn't know it was such a big deal."

"Apparently it is. He said there were lots of family and friends there."

"Well, you know how it is, with just me and Tyler to cover the county it's –"

"Oh, I remember now. We couldn't go because you were too busy. Maybe since I seem to be the sheriff's widow, I just need to get used to doing things by myself."

Tired from all that I had dealt with today, I turned Ellen's words back on her, "Someday, you might just get the chance to try that out."

I'd expected by me pointing out the potential for what she'd said to become a reality that there would be immediate contrition on her part, but she said, "There's leftover beef stew in the fridge. You want me to heat some up for you?"

My stubbornness, however, would not allow me to accept her peace offering, I said, "No thanks, I believe I'll just make myself a peanut butter sandwich and have a beer, maybe two."

She looked at me. Her eyes held a hint of anger but, more than anything, they appeared to want only to escape the conversation, which was probably best, she said, "I'm going to watch tv." And with that she went into the living room. I could hear the music for Mission Impossible come on as I took a Budweiser out of the fridge. I made my sandwich and along with some chips had my supper at the kitchen table. There was a lot to think about, none of it good. Near the end of Mission Impossible, I got a second beer and went into the living room. I took a seat on the couch beside Ellen and we made our apologies to one another, but as we did, I wondered, and I suspect she did too, how long would it be before we would be repeating this scene.

CHAPTER TWENTY-ONE

I'd thought, or rather I'd hoped that Sunday would be a day for our family to be together. As it turned out, Roy got in late the night before after his mother and I had gone to bed, and didn't get up the next morning until almost eleven o'clock. But it was like he said, in the Marines sleep was hard to come by and it was a treat to get to sleep in. So, I did not begrudge him this time. However, the bad part was, not long after he got up dispatch called. Tyler had been sent to a vehicle accident earlier and now there was another wreck about 30 miles north of town. Ellen walked me out to my truck, she said, "Be safe." And then she gave me a kiss.

I said, "I'll be home as soon as I can."

As it turned out the wreck involved two cars, one trying to pass on a hill. Even with the highway patrol's help it took a long time to deal with it all. There were two fatalities and three serious injuries. One of the fatalities was a little girl about six, I guess. And then there was the notification. They were local people. It seemed logical that job should go to me.

It was almost five o'clock when I started down Yellow Dog Road. Well before I got to the house, I could see that Roy's car was gone. I instantly felt bad. *Did he not care to spend time with me?*

Ellen came out through the garage as I got out of my pickup. I said, "Where's Roy?"

"His girlfriend's parents are having a barbecue."

"You know, I was thinking this morning that we could do that today, have your mom over, make it family a deal."

"Well, you should have said something."

"I was going to –"

"And then you got called out, I know, Andy, I know."

"I guess we still can."

"It'd be just you, me and mom."

"Emma's gone too."

"Yeah, that friend Barbara of hers came and got her. Said they were going for a soda and drag main."

I snorted and said in a joking way, "Well, the hell with it then. Let's get your mom and ride into the Coffee Cup and have supper. I ain't had nothing to eat since breakfast."

Ellen smiled, "Are you going to change first?"

"I am, for the next couple of hours I'm Joe Blow citizen."

Ellen took hold of my hand and we walked back inside. In less than ten minutes we were in our car, Ellen sitting next to me in the front and Niko in back. Niko said, "I think the special tonight is prime rib."

I glanced up into the rear-view mirror so as to make eye contact, "I hope so. They've got great prime rib."

Ellen said, "Well, since Andy's buying, I think I'm going to have steak and shrimp."

I laughed. "What? I thought you were. Seriously, I didn't bring my wallet."

I kept a straight face for a few seconds before we all laughed. And then when the laughter had died away, I blurted out, "You've got to be shittin' me. I don't believe it."

Ellen looked to where my eyes were focused, she said, "What's the matter?"

A blue van with a red, white and blue peace symbol painted on the side of it had just pulled out. It was coming towards us in the opposite lane. As we passed one another, I looked over at the driver. He smiled and flashed me the peace sign and, in that moment, my mind went back to the day at the jail and the hippy that had thrown up in his cell and was later pissing people off with his singing. It was Jericho. Had I been in uniform and in my pickup, I would have turned around and chased him down, but I was barely into my two hours of being Joe Blow Citizen. I sighed and said, "At some point, I need to talk to that guy."

I tried to not let this chance sighting of Jericho ruin my supper, but I would be lying if I said that I wasn't distracted.

Although I was tired, I wanted to spend some time with Roy as I knew tomorrow would be a busy day with my interviews at the school. I'd purposely stayed up after the ten o'clock news watching John Wayne in the Sands of Iwo Jima. Ellen lasted about 15 minutes into it and then she kissed me goodnight and went to bed. The movie was nearly over when I heard Roy coming in through the garage. Moments later he appeared in the living room entrance. He said, "You're burning the midnight oil."

I looked over and uttered a brief laugh. "Yeah, had to see if the Marines win."

Roy grinned. "And how many times have you seen this?"

"Three or four."

Roy sat down on the couch. "I remember when I was a kid us watching it together. It's always been one of my favorite movies."

"Mine too."

"It's a big deal in the Corps' history."

"I imagine so. I've always been in awe of those guys riding in a landing craft towards a beach where as soon as that gate drops down, they could be shot to pieces. Takes a lot of guts to do that."

Roy nodded while looking at the tv as if he really was interested in what John Wayne was going to do next and then he said, "I know I've never told you but I've always been proud of who you are."

I felt myself choke up a little, "Being sheriff?"

"Yeah, I think it takes a lot of guts to do what you do. Just look at that run-in you had with that sheep herder last fall. That really scared mom. It scared us all."

At first, I thought to respond with some kind of false bravado like, *you've been talking with your mother too much*, but I was truthful, "It scared the hell out of me too." And then I added, "It's not easy to live with killing somebody."

"You didn't have a choice, Dad."

"When you get to Vietnam, you won't either."

Roy sighed just as a Marine on the tv opened up with a Tommy gun and mowed down several Japanese soldiers and said, "I guess I'll cross that bridge when I come to it."

"I doubt that you've seen Owen Bolander since you've been back, but he's a changed person. I hope you don't change like that."

"Since he's been back a lot has happened to him."

"I mean before all of this business with his father and brother. The fun-loving kid that I saw at high school football games has gotten lost somewhere."

Roy shook his head and then shrugged, he said, "I can't say how I'll be when I come back."

"Oh, I know. We'll love you, however you are."

Roy looked over at the tv and was quiet for a few seconds before he looked at me and said, "I just don't want to let my fellow Marines down. When it comes time, I hope I'm not a coward."

I said, "I know you, Roy, and there's not a bit of doubt in my mind that you'll do what's expected of you, and in a way, knowing where you're going, that scares me."

Roy looked at me and grinned weakly. "Scares me too."

We both laughed in a nervous way. I said, "You'll do fine."

And then the national anthem came on the television followed by the Indian chief test pattern. A message that normal broadcasting would resume tomorrow morning at

6:00 a.m. was on the screen as well as being accompanied by a high-pitched noise. Although I turned the tv off, we continued to talk about fishing and hunting and high school sports and his girl friend and guy things until almost 1:30 in the morning. It was a good talk.

CHAPTER TWENTY-TWO

At about a quarter till ten, I parked in front of the Gros Ventre County high school. It was a one story U-shaped red brick building located on the south side of Fremont. The longest side of the U faced Third Street, which in one more block to the north, intersected Main Street. Kids from the Gros Ventre River valley, as well as all of the ranch kids on this side of the mountains, were bussed into Fremont for grades seven through twelve. Those ranch kids in grades 1-6 attended rural elementary schools closer to home. Naturally, the high school with close to 400 students, had the biggest enrollment, how many of them had attended the party at the Cottonwood campground was, hopefully, what I was about to find out.

Judging by the head swivels I'd gotten as I entered the building, I figured that Emma, as well as a large percentage of the other kids, would know I was there by the time the bell rang at ten. As it turned out, the vice-principle was not at school today so I was allowed to use his office. However, it was like being in a fishbowl. It had large windows all the way around. It gave new meaning to the concept of transparency. I had brought a pen and tablet and had just made myself comfortable at a small table in front of the desk when the student aide, a shy blonde-haired girl, who seemed intimidated by my presence, returned with Robby Schultz. Robby, on the other hand, appeared resentful to my being there as he slouched into a padded chair across the table from me. He immediately slid a piece of blue line tablet paper in my direction. He was grinning, which I thought strange until I looked at the list.

I said angrily, "What is this crap, Robby?"

His grin turned into defiance, "Ask her, there's plenty of people that saw her there." He paused and then he laughed, "She gets around, Sheriff."

Anger exploded within me. I wanted to punch him in his smart mouth or at a minimum, curse at him, but I was in the fishbowl. So, I sat there staring at the paper wondering if Bernie Schultz knew what his kid had done and not wondering, but knowing, that the principle and the student aide and the office secretary and the two kids that were coming to school late were all looking into the fishbowl and could tell that the first name on the list was, Emma Yarnell. In a way, I suddenly felt inferior to Robby, unable to defend myself against this snot-nosed kid. "I said, barely glancing at him, "You can go back to class." Feeling victorious, I'm sure, he said nothing more but got up. From the corner of my eye, I could see the smirk on his face but I did not call him on it. Instead, I sat there for a few minutes, pretending to read over the list of names while I processed my disappointment and looked to where the blame should go. After a time, I went to the door and said to the student aide, "Do you know my daughter?"

She nodded, "Emma?"

"Yes, will you go get her?"

Either the girl did not realize the gravity of what I'd just asked or it came as no surprise to her that my daughter would be called in for questioning. She nodded, "Ok, it'll be just a minute while I look up her file."

I went back into the fish bowl and sat down. The last names of many of the kids on the list, I recognized. There were 42 of them, all from mostly good families, Robby

Schultz being one of the exceptions. In a way, this made me feel a little better about Emma being on the list. I wanted to believe that Robby was lying about her, *getting around,* but would he say that just to spite me? I was staring at the list, deep in anticipation of what I might learn about my daughter, when the door opened and Emma came in. Although she closed the door behind her I knew there would be no hiding the Yarnell family's dirty laundry, not now, not here in the fish bowl. Her face said she knew about the list and mine, ever the open book, said how disappointed I was that her name was on it. Neither of us spoke as she took a seat in the same chair that Robby had occupied. To her credit, her eyes had become watery, she said, "I'm sorry, Dad."

I hesitated, knowing that the effects of what I said might never go away, finally, I said, "Did you have fun?"

Some of the apprehension in her face appeared to melt, she said, "At first I did, but later not."

"Why is that?"

"People just got too drunk and crazy. Some got sick and were throwing up and there was a fight. It just got to be not fun."

"The fight, was that between Billy Stroud and Owen Bolander?"

"Yes, but it was mostly yelling and some shoving and then people stopped them."

"So, how'd you get to the party?"

It was clear she did not want to say but, finally, she said, "Tommy Dunn took me."

"I thought you were with your friend Barbara that night."

"For a while I was, but then we ran into Tommy and he wanted us to go to the party."

"Barbara didn't go?"

Emma shook her head as if to stir her shame. "No, she went home."

The father in me couldn't help but draw the comparison, "Why didn't she go?"

Embarrassment overtook Emma's face, she said, "It was pretty clear Tommy didn't want her to go."

Robby's words, *she gets around*, echoed in my mind but, at the same time, I could feel the eyes outside the fishbowl looking in. I knew the direction the conversation was going was more about the moral character of my daughter and less about the murder of Billy Stroud. Nonetheless, I pushed on, "Was Tommy drinking at this party?"

Emma looked at me, her eyes having become more defensive, "Yes. Dad, he was."

In that instant, my mind went back a couple of years ago to a wreck involving three teenagers, a souped-up car and too much beer. They missed a curve and rolled twice. The force was such that the entire engine was separated from the car. All of them were killed. I said, "You know, Emma, I can understand your wanting to experiment with all of this but bear in mind, you're playing with fire."

Emma nodded, "I know, it's just, well, there were a lot of other kids there."

"I realize that, but teenage boys often times don't have logical thoughts."

"Tommy's a good kid."

"Well, I know you and your mother have talked about these things."

"Dad, it wasn't like that."

"Ok, I didn't mean to lecture you. I just have a couple of more questions though."

"Do you know a long-haired guy by the name of Jericho?"

"I don't know him, but I know who he is."

"Did you see him at the party?"

"Yeah, he was there."

"You ever see him interact with Owen or Billy?"

Emma was thoughtful for a moment and then said, "I believe he was talking to Billy early on but after that, I don't know."

"You wouldn't happen to know where this guy lives would you?"

"C'mon, Dad, how would I know that?

"I just thought you might have heard something."

Emma sighed. "You might talk to Melissa Hargroves. I've heard she's been out with Jericho. Her name should be on the list."

I scanned down the names, "Yeah, it is."

"Talk with her but don't mention my name. It's going to be bad enough as it is."

"I'm sorry, I hope this investigation won't cause trouble for you."

"It'll be the dopers that'll be the most freaked out about it."

"That include Robby and Melissa?"

Emma looked around, as if it wasn't already too late, to see who might be listening outside the fishbowl, she said, "Yeah, big time." She paused, "And yes, Dad, I've tried pot but I don't care for it."

I gave a gentle laugh, "Well, I guess now that you've had your morning confession you can go back to class."

Emma smiled. "I love you, Dad."

"I love you too."

CHAPTER TWENTY-THREE

As it turned out, Melissa had been recently dumped by Jericho who, according to her, prided himself on being some kind of stud. She had been to his place a couple of times, but even more interesting was the picture he had shown her of him in his karate attire. She'd said, *he brags a lot about being a black belt.*

Around 11:30 I left the high school and went to my truck. I keyed my radio, "Cummins/Yarnell."

"Go ahead, Andy."

"Tyler, I need for you to go with me up to Goldberg."

"Right now, I was going to meet my girl for lunch."

"Sorry, but this is important. Meet me at the rest stop north of town and I'll explain."

"Alright, I'll be there in about five minutes."

The rest stop, which was about two miles outside of town, had actually started out as a historical site with parking for a half dozen cars and a sign telling how trappers in the early 1800's would rendezvous here and trade with the Indians. Some years ago, the state put in a rest room. It had no water, just facilities to do your business. Nonetheless, its presence overshadowed the trappers that had been here a hundred and fifty years ago and the place was now best known for the relief it afforded someone needing to take a leak. Tyler was leaning against his car with his arms folded across his chest when I pulled up. Since I'd hired him a little over a year ago, our relationship had grown to where we both felt comfortable with him saying to me, "So, what the hell is so important that I've got to miss lunch with a pretty girl and go galivanting off to beautiful downtown Goldberg with a crusty old guy like you?"

"Jericho lives out there."

"How'd you come to know this?"

"An ex-girlfriend. Said he lives in a little log shack about a quarter mile north of the store."

"Oh, I think I know the place you're talking about. It kinda sits back in the trees."

I nodded. "We need to be careful with this guy. Supposedly, he's some kind of karate tough, got a black belt according to his girlfriend."

"You thinkin' he killed the Stroud kid?"

"Well, right now he seems like a better candidate than Owen."

"So, we're just going there to have a chat?"

"Yup, just a friendly chat and if that's going ok, I'm gonna ask to see the bottom of his shoes."

"And what if he won't show us his shoes?"

"Well, I'm hoping there's some soft dirt near his cabin."

"And if there is?"

I smiled. "That's why your along."

Tyler did not smile or laugh as I had expected. His eyes were pretty well hidden beneath his gray Stetson and behind his aviator sunglasses. He was a little over six feet and muscular, but he seemed to have a healthy respect for the hippy being a karate expert as I could sense his fear, he said, "I guess we'll just see how it goes."

"Well, the city boys arrested him last fall when he was falling down drunk but today will probably be a different story."

Tyler nodded, "I'll be on my toes."

"Oh, by the way, I checked with Bee over at the jail to see what Jericho's real name is." I paused and grinned, "turns out it's Buford Leroy Perkins."

The usual Tyler came back. He laughed, "No wonder this guy got a black belt. Buford Leroy, what kind of parents would name their kid that?"

I laughed, "I don't know if I should call him by his real name or not, that might start a fight right there."

Tyler laughed and I did too again. It helped to disguise our fear.

Goldberg was a smaller version of Cedarville. It was located in the bottom of a steep sided canyon. Several old mine shafts were still visible on the slopes to either side of town, but the bulk of the scars to the land were hidden by the trees and brush that had re-grown in the ninety years since there was any significant mining. The little village struggled to survive. Last year they were going to close the post office that's located in a tiny room inside the general store. But the store owner wrote his congressman and told him if the post office closed, the store, along with its gas pump would go under and so today, the American flag still flies out front. Across the gravel road from it was the Owl bar and café.

It was almost 12:30 when Tyler and I slowly rolled into the commercial part of Goldberg. To our left was the store. It was built from rough cut pine boards that were badly in need of staining. Black tarpaper that was frayed in many places covered the roof and surrounded a rusty tin stovepipe. Blue smoke was drifting up from it as there was still snow high on the mountains. Big red letters on a white background that were barely legible occupied a façade above the porch overhang, they read: GOLDBERG STORE. The store owner, an old man with white hair and moustache, was sitting in a brown padded chair just to the right of the door. Its fabric was worn and tattered but the man, sunk down in it as he was, appeared comfortable. On the wall above him was a metal sign with badly chipped letters advertising Shasta pop. The man, whose name was Walter Kozak, was staring at me to the point I felt compelled to stop and talk. He got up out of his chair and came over next to my pickup. He said, "I been wonderin' when you were gonna show up out here."

I said, resting the crook of my arm out my truck's window, "Why's that?"

"Well, I'd be willing to bet you're going up to that damned hippie's place, ain't ya?"

"I take it you think we should be."

He snorted, "Ain't nobody out here that needs arresting but him. That is why yer here, ain't it?"

I said, "Do you know, is there anybody besides Jericho at his place?"

Walter reached into the hip pocket of his bib overalls and pulled out a foil packet of Red Man chewing tobacco, as he did he said, "I can't say for sure about today, but generally there's a fair number of people that come and go from that place." He paused to put a good-sized pinch of tobacco in his mouth and then he went on, "There's seedy looking people that goes all hours of the day up there. Not long ago, there was this motorcycle gang come to town."

"A gang"

"There was a half dozen of 'em I'd guess. They had these jackets that said they was from Billings. They stopped here on their way back from ole thimble dick's place and filled up with gas."

I laughed, "Thimble dick?"

Walter turned to the side and spit an arcing stream of tobacco juice back near my rear tire. He dabbed at his moustache with the knuckles of his right hand and then went on, "He thinks he's a real ladies' man so that's what I call him."

"I assume not to his face?"

"Oh, hell no. That kid's not right in the head. I don't know if it's just all those left-handed cigarettes he smokes or if he was wired wrong from the git-go, but I wouldn't turn my back on him if I was you. He runs with a rough crowd, Sheriff."

I nodded, "Alright, Walter, I appreciate the heads up." I drove on, with Tyler in tow. My heart was racing. I told myself that today wasn't going to be a repeat of that day up Badger Creek. And, at the same time, I wondered if stopping to talk with Walter hadn't been such a good idea. Everything seemed to matter now, like I was seeing it for the last time. We went past the Owl bar and café, past an old ramshackle clapboard house with a '52 pea green Chevy coupe sitting out front and a round tub washing machine laying on its side. Not far away, and across the road, was a log house with a caved in roof. Just beyond it was a single wide cream-colored trailer with a black International pickup next to it, and then, we rounded a slight bow in the road and there was not only Jericho's cabin but Jericho himself, standing out front. I parked beside his van and got out. Tyler stopped behind my truck. There would be no time to tell him what Walter had said as Jericho was walking towards me. I took a few steps in his direction and then froze just short of a patch of floury dirt.

Jericho called out in a voice that was close to sarcasm, "I'm assuming you fellas aren't here for lunch."

My eyes had fallen away to the soft dirt in front of me. I could see without kneeling that the track there had the same rectangle as the track where Billy had been killed. In that instant, I knew the chances were good that I'd be arresting Jericho. I looked up. "Afternoon, Jericho."

A surprised look came to his face. "How is it you know my name?"

From the corner of my eye, I saw that Tyler had come up on my right but slightly behind me. I said, "We've been talking to people that were at a party out in the Gros Ventre at the Cottonwood campground. Your name came up as someone who was there."

"So, what if I was?"

"Well, there was lots of drinking going on by minors."

"I didn't have anything to do with that."

Tyler said, "We heard too that people were smoking pot. You know anything about that?"

Anger suddenly came to Jericho's eyes. "You know, I'm getting tired of being hassled by you guys. You need to go look elsewhere because I personally didn't see anybody smoking weed at that party, at least not while I was there."

I said, "Well, what time did you leave the party?"

"I don't remember."

"Did you happen to talk to Billy Stroud while you were there?"

"No, I-" he paused sensing that he was about to be caught in a lie and said, "yeah, I talked to Billy."

Tyler said, "What did you talk about?"

"Nothing much."

I said, "You know that somebody killed him?"

Jericho feigned mild surprise. "Really, I hadn't heard."

I played along, "I guess clear out here news travels slow."

Tyler said, "So, you two didn't argue about anything?"

"Not me, talk to that Bolander guy. He's the one that got into it with Billy. I left kinda early so I don't know what all went on out there."

I said, "I thought you didn't remember when you left."

He shot me a dirty look as he put both his hands in the pouch pocket of the hooded sweatshirt that he was wearing. He said again, "Why do you guys keep hassling me?"

I said, almost on top of Jericho's words, "Take your hands out of your pocket."

"C'mon man, it's cold."

And then I saw, through the cloth, his right hand maneuvering, I yelled, "Gun." But it was too late. It was like firecrackers going off, that little .25 caliber automatic. It took just one, not even as loud as a big black cat, that penetrated the right lens of Tyler's aviator sunglasses. He went down instantly and without a sound. I, on the other hand, yelled, "Oh, shit," about the time the next bullet struck me high in the right side of my chest. It felt like a heavy thud that didn't move me much and then, I swear, just for a millisecond, I had the feeling or thought that, *well, that wasn't so bad.* But then another firecracker went off and I felt some pain, this time in my gut. My knees started to buckle. Fortunately, my right hand hadn't been caught up in the hysteria and had continued on to my holster. The beauty of a double action Colt .38, as I had learned with Joe Garmendia, was there is no safety to release or round to be chambered, just pull the trigger, which I did almost simultaneous to Jericho pulling his. I felt another thud on the other side of my chest just above my heart. Jericho tried to shoot me again but the bullet went a little wide of my face and then he dropped his gun and staggered in a confused way for a few seconds before he fell down. I knew, or so I hoped, that he was dead because he just laid there, his right cheek in the dirt but his eyes wide open, staring at me. Nonetheless, I kept a tight grip on my pistol until a little gust of wind blew some of the floury dirt into his eyes. He did not blink. I felt some relief in this and relaxed the grip on my .38 while looking away to Tyler. It was an effort, as my breathing was rattling, gurgling almost, I called out, "Tyler, can you hear me? Tyler." But he was quiet and still as stone. I strained to hear, thinking maybe he was trying to whisper. There was the caw of a raven flying overhead and the gentle moan of the wind in the tops of the pine trees and then nothing but the beating of my heart and the rattle in my lungs. I knew just by the way he was laying, kind of crumpled up, face down in the dirt, that he was gone. I felt bad, guilty for asking him to come here with me. He should be in town eating lunch with his girl. But then

I thought of the criticism I'd gotten for not taking someone with me when I confronted Garmendia. Anger instantly boiled up within me. It was a no-win situation, a *what if I hadn't called him* scenario that I knew I would be replaying in my mind for a long time to come. And then I thought, *but what if I die? Tyler and I will be wherever it is dead people go and we'll be able to discuss what we did wrong today. He'll be free to tell me then if he's mad at me.* But suddenly, Ellen appeared in my mind. Before I left the fish bowl, I had called her and asked for a raincheck on lunch. As usual, she was understanding. The thought of how she'd be if someone was to come to her and say that I was dead, caused me to try and get up. But it was like I had a heavy blanket over me, I just couldn't do it. I knew that I had to get to the radio in my pickup or I would die, but it felt so good to rest my head in some green grass and look up at the clouds. I told myself, *I'll rest a minute and then I'll crawl to my truck.*

It was fortunate that a forest service guy, a co-worker of Ellen's, came down the canyon. He saw the vehicles in front of Jericho's cabin. They caused him to slow down and look to see what the law was doing at the hippie's cabin. He almost didn't notice the bodies on the ground, but then he did. The doctor said it was good that he saw me when he did and that he had the moxie to stop and walk up on three bodies, not knowing if he might end up like them. I wasn't aware that he had found me and called for help until I was on a helicopter going to Great Falls. At the time, I didn't know that Ellen had heard all of the radio traffic including, *the Sheriff's deputy is dead and he's not far behind.* She collapsed right there in the front office. Thank God Roy had been home. He brought the family, including Bella, to Great Falls. That had been five days ago. Owing to the fact that I was mostly out of the woods everyone but Ellen. had gone home yesterday. I'd told them to go. They had commitments of work, school and a war to go to and they knew as well as I did that it wouldn't be cheap staying on.

It was a couple of minutes past eight when Ellen stepped into my room. "Good morning, how'd you sleep?"

I looked up and met her lips before saying, "They keep me so doped up it's hard not to sleep."

"Well, like they say, sleep heals all and you've got lots of healing to do."

I looked at the IV in the back of my hand and the alligator clip on my finger with a wire leading to a monitor by my bed. I said, "Did the doctor say when he thinks I can get out of here?"

"Maybe in another week."

"A week?"

"At the earliest. Andy, you've got to remember that you lost a lot of blood. You've got a bullet hole in your liver and your right lung and another inch lower you would've had one in your heart."

I forced a smile. "Well, on the bright side, if Jericho had been a better shot, I wouldn't be laying here eating hospital food and using a bedpan."

Ellen frowned. "Stop it, Andy."

"Sorry."

Ellen's expression brightened. "You're a celebrity. The paper here had a write up on what happened. I meant to bring it."

"Maybe tomorrow."

"It said mostly what you already know that the highway patrol found almost 20 pounds of marijuana, some cocaine, LSD, over $15,000 in cash and a number of guns"

"It's a good thing Jericho is no longer part of society."

"But, at what price, Andy? Tyler's dead and you nearly were."

I sighed. "It is a heavy price."

Ellen looked hard into my eyes, she said, "This family is done. There's not going to be anymore Jerichos or Joe Garmendias. Promise me Andy, you're going to retire."

I'd always thought that retiring would be difficult, but the words came surprisingly easy, "I promise."

EPILOGUE

August 10, 1966

Truth be told, retirement agreed with me as I never really felt quite right after the shooting. Having a hole in one of my lungs and my liver kind of took the wind out of my sails. But I felt good enough to ride a tractor or swather for a few days here and there for different ranchers. I didn't make much money at this but with my early medical retirement and Ellen's salary and tightening our belts a little, we were getting by. In fact, life was good. We made plans to do things and actually stuck to it. Emma was getting ready to go over to Bozeman to college and Roy, so far, hadn't seen a lot of action in Vietnam.

But then came the day that Ellen and I met for lunch at the Coffee Cup. They were busy and, as luck would have it, in walks Owen and Norma Bolander. The only available table was next to ours. I could see from across the room that Norma wanted to leave but Owen wouldn't have it. He put his hand in the small of her back and pushed her a step or two in our direction. The waitress seated them not five feet from us. The last I'd talked to Owen or Norma, for that matter, was right after Billy Stroud's murder. For a time, it was like a white elephant had parked itself between our tables and nobody wanted to recognize it. I assumed they didn't want to talk to me in light of all that had happened in the past. But then, Norma said, "Andy, how are you doing?"

I looked over at her, "I'm doing alright. I guess you know I'm not the sheriff anymore." I paused, uncertain if I should ask but then I did, "And you, how are you faring?"

Norma's eyes looked sad and tired. Strangely, Owen seemed content to let his mother do the talking. She said, her voice beginning to falter, "We're getting by."

I'd been told different, but I said, "I'm glad to hear that." And then Owen crossed his right leg over his left knee exposing the bottom of his shoe. My pulse quickened. I hoped this was one time when my face didn't read like an open book. Fortunately, the waitress came to take their order.

After a time, while we were driving to where we were going to fish, I told Ellen what I had seen. She listened patiently until I was done, but then she said, "You promised, Andy." And then she looked out the window.

www.ingramcontent.com/pod-product-compliance
Lightning Source LLC
Chambersburg PA
CBHW031631130726
47900CB00019B/2404